Splashes of Ma

(A Fictional Account of Sibling Rivalry)

BY YINKA ADEBOYE

SPLASHES OF MANY COLORS

(A Fictional Account of Sibling Rivalry)

YINKA ADEBOYE

Splashes of Many Colors

(A Fictional Account of Sibling Rivalry)

By Yinka Adeboye

The author can be reached at fiyinka3@yahoo.com.

ISBN-13:978-1985640177

ISBN-10:1985640171

Note to Reader

The author acknowledges the songs used in this book:

**Que Sera Sera*-- by Doris Day

**I Bless the Day I found You*-- by Everly Brothers

**I will Always Love You*-- by Whitney Houston

*Thank You, Lord, for Your Blessings-- by Jeff & Sheri Easter

**Devoted to You*-- by Everly Brothers

By The Same Author

*Rumblings of My Inner Thoughts (Poetry)

*God: A Consuming Fire

*It is So Long

*Lemon with Pride

*Entangled Web (a Play)

*Selected African Stories my Grandma Told Me

Dedication

This work is affectionately dedicated to all those vulnerable people who survived sibling rivalry in their developing years.

It could have been worse, if not for the mercy of the Almighty God.

Table of Content

Acknowledgment

I am greatly indebted to this great visionary and philanthropist, Dr Wale Okediran; the CEO and Patron of The EBEDI INTERNATIONAL WRITERS' RESIDENCY program, who gave me the opportunity to be one of the selected few for the highly competitive and prestigious six-week residency program.

The serenity and beautiful location of Ebedi International Writers' Residency in Iseyin Oyo State Nigeria, gave me the comfort, peace and tranquility that writers crave for, far from the hurly-bustling of the maddening crowd. I delightfully and generously capitalized on the opportunity to churn out a number of published works.

I am profoundly grateful to Chief Oladejo Okediji who is like a father indeed and a mentor in this literary world. He has been a great blessing to me through his constant pieces of advice. To Mr. Moses A. Olowe, for his goodwill at all times. I am most grateful.

My heart goes with tremendous thanks most especially to my childhood friend, Bashorun (Dr.) Dele Momodu. He is a man of varied career who is a teacher, a journalist, a writer, an author, an entrepreneur, an inspiration to the youth, a politician, a business man, an excellent example of humility, an enigma, a man whose philanthropy is rare to find, an Administrator and the Publisher of the high profile Ovation Magazine. Dele is ever supportive of me; always encouraging me and spurring me on, to be the best I could be in this make-believe world of my profession. Thank you, Dele.

I must also acknowledge and appreciate these gentlemen, Tunji Fatilewa, Bayode Oluwasanmi, and Adekunle Adepitan (KP). Their support throughout the duration of writing this book is well treasured.

Special mention must be made of my Cousin, John Adebisi Adeyefa and of my dear friends, Olakunle Afilaka, Henri T De

Souza and Mrs Olabisi Amoke Marinho. Their input and bringing their wealth of experiences to bear in this work is highly acknowledged and appreciated. I want to say a big thank you to them.

To all my friends who have been there for me all along in prayers and goodwill while at the program; Rev'd. Tunji Akintayo, Mrs. Adebola Esuruoso Fashanu, Mrs. Ibiyemi Ilesanmi, Mr. Muri Awoseemo and Ms Bukola Adeleke; I say thank you all.

My sincere and heartfelt gratitude goes to Mr. Akin Ajayi-Obe. You have been a great blessing to me in many ways. I celebrate and thank you Sir!

I recognize and treasure my siblings… Thank you for this robust support system I get at all times from you… a standing ovation to them; Dr. (Mrs.) Biola Molokwu, Mrs. Shola Emeghara, Mrs. Adedunni Awoyemi and Pastor (Engr.) Paul Oluwole Adeyeoluwa. I cannot exchange you for anything in this world! Thank you all.

And to Dr. Fiyinfoluwa Adeboye; thank you for standing strong, for being selfless and for being the best that you are! I value the bond we share. God will honor you, my Darling. Love you lots!

To all my readers; this is a good story. I hope you will enjoy it. God bless! Thank you all.

Yinka Adeboye (née Adeyefa)

Praise for the novel of Splashes of Many Colors

"An enchanting and heartwarming story... Surprisingly different...!"---Prophet Folayan Osekita... United Kingdom.

"This wonderful family story is just what you need to read!"---Prince Oriade Adeoye ...Lagos, Nigeria.

"Yet again; Yinka Adeboye delivers"! --- Olori Olubunmi Faleti...Ibadan, Nigeria.

"Intriguing...A compulsive readable novel... Yinka is a story teller who can hold her readers spellbound. Her latest book makes a compelling reading"! ---Mr. Akin Ajayi-Obe...Ilesa Nigeria.

Author's Note

I rose to be who I am today in the world of make-believe fiction on the shoulders of my wonderful siblings. One way or the other, each one of them is part of my success story.

When I was younger and in the primary school, my older sisters, Biola and Shola took turns to buy comics for me to read. Little did I know that they were whetting my appetite towards the world of fiction! My interest in story books grew in leaps and bounds thereafter. I became a voracious reader and my sense of imagination was sharpened.

As I grew older in my teenage years, my childhood friend, Bashorun Dele Momodu, the Publisher of Ovation magazine took over the responsibility of exchanging so many of his novels with mine. He made sure I became a fast reader just like him.

However, the act of storytelling that I imbibed was birthed in me by my mother's elder Sister, Late Mrs. C.O. Somide whom we fondly called Mamae. She it was who told me and the other children in her guardianship, so many moonlight stories and many of such indigenous stories were figments of her imagination. I started "weaving" stories together just as she did.

The story in this book is another one of make-believe first narrative stories I have weaved together to make it seem real. Abayomi, the hero in this heart wrenching story was able to recount the vicissitude of his life; he was telling his story without any mix-up. He suffered an unimaginable psychological and physical abuse in the hands of his elder brother who saw him as a rival.

The sibling rivalry is an age long phenomenon in which almost all families could relate with. In some families the occurrences could be very fierce, alarming and life threatening while in others there could be pockets of bickering here and there which they would easily resolve within themselves.

The act of rivalry could be friendly without animosity. It encourages the people involved to strife harder to do much better. If such rivalry is not healthy it could lead to hatred or loss of lives. However, not all sibling hostility ends in murder plots.

There are people whose siblings remain life-long friends and confidants. Those ones are considered as being favored. There are also other people who have to tolerate the resentments, betrayer, envy and wickedness of their siblings.

When anyone is going through this type of stress, they should endeavor to seek help and speak out. It is so important knowing that there's someone in your life who you can talk with about anything. Unfortunately, there are people who couldn't cope with the monumental stress and they had to commit suicide.

I spent a lot of time thinking about how to write this story without making it seem as if I was all out to antagonize any individual. In one sense, I wanted to showcase the fact that when there is a strong will, there is a way in life. And in another deeper sense, I wanted those who are undergoing sibling rivalry to learn how to move on with their lives irrespective of what they might be going through. There is always light at the end of the tunnel.

It is important to mention that, I am observant of my surroundings and I have learned from those around me that the lasting value in sibling relationship is love.

Yinka Adeboye.

Chapter 1

The Invitation

From the look of the invitation card I held in my hands, I was able to see that the party was going to be an outstanding and a dazzling one. It was printed in gold and rimmed with velvet strap. The card read, *"This card admits a couple."* I had kept my copy so jealously because that was my only assurance of stepping into the prestigious BAMMY HALL.

The party couldn't have taken place anywhere else aside of BAMMY Hall which can sit 4,000 guests. The gigantic masterpiece with beautiful ambience is located on Challenge road Ibadan, Nigeria. It is only hired out to the High and Mighty of the society because of its rental fee that amounts to millions of Naira. So when I got an invite to Chief Banji Ayobamidele Madu's 60th Birthday bash, I held the card with both hands. I was so delighted that I had gone to the moon and back. I could not keep still; I felt I was 10feet tall. It is not every day that one gets to mingle with celebrities, captains of industries, the royal dignitaries, the military as well as the politicians.

My acquaintance with Banji Madu dated back to our secondary school days in Ile-Ife. I attended Our Lady's Girls' High School while Banji went to St. John's Grammar School. Our Schools have affiliation with one another being Catholic schools.

We lived on the same Road at the University Quarters and saw each other regularly during the holidays. We became close friends when we were placed in the same class at the inception of a Summer Holiday Couching Classes in Ile-Ife inside Oduduwa College premises in 1974. So many students from different schools converged there for the one month holiday coaching classes.

It was like a magnet as Banji and I stuck together. He is like the kind of brother I had always wanted to have. He did his best to understand me whenever I was feeling low.

There was nothing we didn't share together; laughter, sadness, gist, fear, little secrets, novels... name it...! I used to pour out my mind to him in those days of vulnerability when I needed a shoulder to cry on. He is a great listener, a very patient guy and the owner of a broad shoulder to lean on. He is kind, warm, funny and friendly.

At the time we were growing up, Banji was the one person outside my family who had always believed in me. He knew how to bring me down to earth and he knew the right words to say at the right time. Up until now, I am convinced that he had been on this planet earth before.

I have done more crying and laughing with Banji than anyone else. I don't think there is anything I can't talk to him about. He is the first and the last opinion I value. As far as he is concerned, I don't hold anything back from him. He knows me so well. I still maintain a close and incredibly supportive relationship with him.

His passion for reading novels is overwhelming; one cannot be Banji's friend and not love to read novels. His deep knowledge for writing is amazing and infectious. His recipe for life is... "Be what you want to be"! It was a shock to me that year, when he opted to study the sciences; he was so good in the Humanities. Through sheer talent and determination, Banji had become a household name over the past decades. He is one of the bigwigs in Lagos, Abuja and Ghana social and corporate circles as he is well connected to the seat of Power.

He sits atop some multinational companies and had hit a gold mine and had gone ahead to be a very successful business man in the manufacturing and selling of vehicle tyres. He is also into the manufacturing of ceramic tiles and building accessories. He has become a big man and very wealthy by all standard. I also heard it from the grapevine that he had been given a license to lift crude oil. He has a fast track to fame.

For years, our paths did not meet after he graduated from the University. I left a year ahead of him because he studied a Five-year course in civil engineering and had a First class Honors. It was not until one day that I just saw him out of the blues in Abuja.

I had gone to an office for an official transaction and was sitting down quietly at the reception when a warm hand rested at the back of my neck. I turned immediately. I was not expecting to know anybody around there. It was a huge man in flowing regalia of *agbada,* who called my name in a special way that was reserved only for my special friends;

"*Yinkus mi*"!

I stood up immediately and was piercing into his eyes. Who could it be? He stood there smiling and looking at me admiringly.

It took a few minutes for me to gather my wits about me that it was my dear friend, Banji Ayobamidele Madu, the one I fondly call BJ who was standing right before my very eyes. I screamed in spite of myself; I gave him a bear-hug and held him so tightly remembering those good old days of when we were inseparable.

"Hey..., BJ, is this really you? Banji Madu, am I right?" I asked while searching his face for reassurance.

"*Yinkus mi*, you are still the same old self; I could fish you out in a crowd with my eyes blindfolded." His voice was as clear as a bell and I laughed heartily at his exaggeration.

His face was creased with laughter and a beam of satisfaction spread across his face as he patted me by the cheeks. He asked what I had come to do in that Establishment and held me by the hand as we both moved towards the Minister's office.

"Keep the 16th of May open for me dear, it's my birthday and I am celebrating it in a big way. It's my 60th, you know!" BJ beamed with smiles.

I composed a poem for him in my heart right away, as the old flame of our intimacy was being fanned by our renewed acquaintance.

It is your Birthday my dear friend

A time to celebrate for fun at the fair

A time to jubilate and reflect on the past

At sixty, your wine gets sweeter and tastier

At sixty, heads, still turn at your entrance

At sixty, I feel you are that young boy of sixteen

But now you are that handsome man at sixty!

Chapter 2

The Reunion

From the array of exotic and sophisticated cars that were packed outside the event Hall, I knew that was the place to be! It was a show of class as the latest and customized automobiles were on parade. I had to automatically change my poise and back my step pings to fit the occasion...as they say, when in Rome, do as the Romans. I walked elegantly towards the Hall and stood at the entrance; I let out a sigh, "this is life"! I must enjoy it to the fullest!

The water tight security at the entrance was expected. The whole venue was guarded by professionals and armed security men in black uniforms. The security was so tight that no room was given to any gatecrashers or beggars. Usually, when I enter a hall or any gathering such as this one, I would first pause at the entrance and scan through the room. This is just a gimmick of mine to prepare myself to being confident.

I stepped in with grace and aura. The interior decoration of the BAMMY Hall was heavenly; it was gorgeously transformed with shimmery chandeliers and lovely drapes of chiffon and cotton fabric with lights. The venue was a beauty to behold as decoration was at its best and it was freshly perfumed. The air-conditioned splits were blowing cool air and the music from the band stand was sonorous. Everything looked perfect, glittering and magnificent. I was spell bound!

The beautiful colors of the day were Champaign Gold and Teal Green. Fashion was at its best as guests were stunningly and beautifully dressed. The combinations on guests were very attractive. The men too were in fashion. They wore beautiful well designed outfits and paparazzi were all over them trying to get shots of their stylish ensembles.

I said a small prayer within me to thank God that I decided to put on this lovely attire I bought specially for this occasion. If I had listened to what FM told me, I would have been so self conscious by now. He had said it was a waste of money buying new attires whenever there was a party or an event to attend.

"I don't understand you ladies...," he lamented one day. "... Must you always change your wardrobe at every occasion? Same thing with the shoes and bags; must you replace those ones too? Isn't that a waste of money?"

My darling husband, whom I fondly call FM and he in turn affectionately calls me *Sisi mi,* asked me that question when I told him I was buying a new outfit for BJ's birthday bash. I hurriedly replied him;

"You are a man, so you may not understand that I need to feel good about myself in a new outfit at such a classy gathering. All the "Who is Who" of this country would be in attendance. The color code is Champaign gold with a touch of Teal green."

"Hey...? Champaign what...?" FM looked at me sharply and shook his head slowly.

"Yes, Champaign Gold! The Teal Green color is for the accessories, such as the head-tie, shoes and bag." I explained patiently.

"*Sisi mi*, I just marvel at the way you ladies give names to colors. The other day, you mentioned pepper Red, custard Yellow, turquoise Blue, fuchsia Pink, cockroach Brown and minty Green. Another time, you talked about Magenta, Coral, Peach, Onion, Aqua, Ivory and Plum. Right now, I'm hearing Champaign Gold, Teal Green... Hey? Women...!"

My husband exclaimed elaborately with his hands up.

"Yes...*keh*! I need to look good. What about it?" I asked defensively, rolling my eyeballs up and down.

FM was not in the mood to slug it out with me. He knew it was a war he would never win when it comes to fashion stuff. So he simply waved me away and continued with what he was doing.

However, I went ahead to get myself this lovely head-turning lace material. I made a skirt and a top that showed all my curves. I didn't regret following my heart in taking extra care of dressing up and making over. I must say, I really looked good!

Earlier that morning, I had looked in the mirror and inspected my set of teeth. They were still good and in spite of the tell tale signs of old age of wrinkles and grey hair; I could pass for a younger woman!

****

It didn't take me long to spot the celebrant moving from one table to another, sharing banters and back slapping from his friends and guests. I moved closer to him and was about to tap him at the back when he turned.

"Hey! *Yinkus mi.* Wow...! You look so beautiful..." He beamed at me and gave me a big hug that almost wrapped me up with his *agbada* regalia. I was careful not to stain it with my lipstick and compact face powder.

"Thank you, BJ. Congratulations and Happy Birthday to you! This is really lovely". I said, looking around.

"Where is FM, didn't he come with you?" BJ asked.

"No, we had to split. He has gone to represent us at another function in town and here I am. I would not wish to miss your bash for anything." I replied.

"Thanks dear, I trust you. Let me take you to the table where my friends are." He said.

BJ led the way to a long table that seemed like a high table on itself. I nodded my greetings to a few people I recognized from the Facebook online chat and also from the pages of the newspaper and I felt so conscious of myself being in their midst.

I got a seat facing a good-looking couple. The man looked much older than the woman; something like being old enough to be her father. They were both clad in the same type of very expensive lace material; surely they must be a couple and a wealthy one at that!

My eyes caught the time piece (watch) the man wore on his wrist; it made such a style statement. The one on his wife's wrist too was stylish and stunning.

I settled down quickly and looked at the table set before me. The iced bowls on the tables were filled with different types of exotic spirits and beverages; Moet, Champagne Rose, Whiskey (Johnny Walker), Cognac (Hennessey), Vodka (Ciroc), Gin (Gordon's Dry Gin), Rum (Bacardi), Chateau Unang, Bailey's Irish Cream Whiskey, Red wine, white wine, Sparkling wine, different brands of Beer...and so on.

Guests were pampered endlessly throughout the event with mouth-watering delicacies and alcoholic drinks. I tell you, it has to be seen to be believed!

It seemed like a bottle to one person. There were also different types of carbonated drinks, juice drinks, water and refreshing cocktail. I took a bottle of Pizzorno red wine and poured some in my wine glass cup. The wine was broad and rich, with plenty of dark juicy fruit and a bright acidity. Tables were also filled with different types of delicious meals, from local to continental dishes. Small chops, cake and ice cream were largely served round the tables in surplus. There was so much to eat!

I sampled all the tasty finger food and drinks the party had to offer. Attending parties such as this one is my sweetest pleasure. I was enthralled by the constant flow of edibles to our table. There was no hold bars. My mind went to my determination to control my diet and I felt guilty.

Here was a spreadsheet of pastry and fried pieces of meat put before me and I couldn't believe myself to be entertaining thoughts of watching my weight! What was wrong with me?

This was one of the times I deliberately shift the thoughts of dieting from my mind. How was I to shut my eyes from these delicacies and not have a taste? I decided to eat as much as I could eat, then I would make plans to hit the gym thereafter.

As a matter of fact, I had made countless of resolutions in the past that I would be mindful of what goes into my mouth but I was unable to keep them. I just could not pin myself down to be faithful in healthy eating lifestyle.

I love to laugh and relax at a pleasant party as this one with a nice cool music; and when I am at home, I love reading novels while I munch chin-chin or eat chocolate bars. So, how could anyone be faithful at portion control in a place like this? I have not achieved any scientifically proven result since I started developing a Healthy Lifestyle but a one day indulgence should not spoil the broth.

Back to the party talks; my main meal had not yet been served to me but a nice looking chef with a tall white cap had come to take my orders. As there was nothing else to do, I glanced round at the blink-blink of some of the ladies in the Hall.

We all looked lovely, I must confess. The beautiful usherettes were gorgeously dressed too in beautiful styles and welcomed and attended to all guests accordingly.

I noticed BJ's wife was moving up and down attending to guests to make sure everything went well. Very visible at the party were the Alumni of Great IFE. I beamed a smile at some of them, showing recognition. One could smell the touch of affluence around them as many of them sit atop big conglomerates. BJ had turned the whole party into some kind of Great IFE Reunion party. He had spent weeks on the internet tracking people down and the Invite had instructed us to come with our spouses.

Suddenly, the atmosphere of the Hall got charged. A very tall guest breezed in adorning a bowler hat with a muffler round his neck. Almost everyone on our long table stood up to welcome him. It was as if a royal King or the President of a country had arrived. Necks were being stretched to have a glimpse of the man whose presence commanded so much opulence and respect.

He was the cynosure of all eyes as he went around shaking hands while the chants of "Presido...Presido"....rented the air! It was then I realized that only one person could be accorded such honor... Wole Olaoye! He was the former Student Union President of Great IFE many decades ago.

A chair was immediately arranged for him to sit at the head of the table and he engaged himself in pleasantries. I moved closer to greet him. He smiled broadly on recognizing me and gave me a hug. He said in his deep baritone voice;

"*Yinkus*, it's good to see you...", and I smiled back at him. The MC also recognized him in his announcement.

One thing I can depict out of the honor bestowed upon this Emeritus Students' Union President anywhere he went could be that when he had the opportunity to lead the Student Unionism at the time he did, he managed it very well.

He led the entire student Body with a godly wisdom and understanding like that of Solomon in the Bible and many years afterwards, he is still enjoying the aura! I would just surmise it to be that, it is good to be good; when an opportunity comes knocking, it is only fair to make good use of it.

****

My eyes drifted back to the couple sitting opposite me. I wondered why a very young beautiful lady like that could marry a much elderly man. Each time I glanced at them, I found that the man was staring at me intently. I quickly lowered my gaze.

After a while, I looked up again, this man was still fixing his eyes on me as if he was listening to the news on the TV of my body. I looked away again. I reasoned that the man was trying to bully me with his gaze, or what could account for this gape competition?

This was one thing I didn't enjoy in attending parties without FM. If my husband was here now, would this man be gawping like this at me? Nevertheless, I lowered my gaze and was cleaning my nails; an act that depicted that I was feeling nervous and lonely. I stopped quickly. What was this man doing to me?

Then I brought out my phone and pretended to surf the internet. While I sat there, I was contemplating whether to return the look or ignore him. A better judgment told me to stare back at him. I took a mouthful from my drink and seized the opportunity to glare at him.

What a dare? He was still looking at me intently even though I was gazing back! To rub insult upon injury, a little smile was dancing at the corners of his mouth. I stole a fleeting look at his young looking wife.

Did she realize the effect her husband's smile was having on my nerves? The poor lady was just sitting down there innocently and staring into space while her husband was busy committing adultery of the eyes..!

About time! A waitress brought my food; a plate of Chinese rice and other assorted broth that accompanied it. It was a relief to find something to thrust my attention upon. I tilted forward, shut my eyes and said a short prayer inwardly to bless the food.

I was about scoping the first spoonful of rice into my mouth when this guy stretched his hand across the table to pin my hand down. With a wide grin, he shouted excitedly;

"It is *Yinkus mi,* isn't it"?

I didn't know whether to confirm it or not. My eyes darted to his wife to see how she was taking the scenario. She only flashed me a lovely smile.

"I don't think I've ever met you before o..." was the reply I gave him. I slowly but gently withdrew my hand from underneath his grip. I put both hands on my laps; I didn't want a repeat of his touch.

"No, I couldn't have missed those dimples on your cheeks. Great IFE, aren't you? *Yinkus mi....*! This is you after so many years"! The man said gaily.

It was now my turn to stare hard at him. This must be an Alumnus of UNIFE; someone from my past but I couldn't readily place his face. Only my intimate friends addressed me as *Yinkus mi* while we were on Campus; he must be one of them.

Within minutes, I was scanning through my "old files of friends" in my brain. He was staring at me and beaming excitedly waiting for me to come up with his name. As if reading my mind, he removed his eye glasses and it was then I was able to see him clearly. I should know him.

His face seemed familiar at that instant but I couldn't place where and when I had known him. He was definitely a remarkable individual, one who could be outstanding in a group with his large eyeballs. He was big, strong and sexually attractive. His voice was husky with musical vibrancy; it was as if he had done too much talking the day before, or was just recovering from a severe bout of flu.

Even as he sat down, he looked tall. I had to stop for a minute or two and racked my brain to remember his name. I kept on staring at him, and then it hit me like a brick and came flooding back...!

"Abayomi Durogbajo....! Could this be you?" I exclaimed excitedly.

"Yes...Same and one! I haven't changed, have I"? He stretched his hands towards me and I shook it. He was so excited and it showed.

"Who says you haven't? I found it hard to recognize you, until you removed your glasses." I replied him.

"*Yinkus, Yinkus*! You were not using glasses in school either. I was able to recognize you but not easily. As soon as you came to the table, I knew I had seen the face before; that was why I was staring at you...trying to fix where you fitted. Sorry for doing that, okay? It was not a sign of a good gentleman. Immediately you shut your eyes to bless your food, your picture in IFE at the Forks and Fingers Restaurant just flashed in my mind". He smiled.

"Abayomi...! We called you Abayor back then, didn't we? It is so nice to connect with you again. You left in 1983 didn't you"? I asked.

"Yes I did." Abayor confirmed and turned to the young lady sitting beside him and held her hands. "This is my dear wife, Tunmise; the mother of my children"!

That sounded strange to me. Could there be a dispute in it? What type of an introduction was that? Why did he have to stress that she was the mother of his children? He could have simply said, "Meet my dear wife, Tunmise!"

I turned to the lady and smiled. I greeted her very well and I returned my gaze to my old friend, wondering why a very young girl like that was his wife. Could that not have been a case of child abuse on his part? What about that girl...what's her name again...the *I-go-die* girlfriend he had on Campus at that time? Did they not make it to the altar...?

It seemed as if Abayor was reading my mind. He said; "*Yinkus mi...*I know what you are thinking about. Mary-Anne and I did not make it to the altar. Incredible, isn't it? We were an item back then on the Campus!"

All I could do was to nod my head and I stylishly squinted at the young wife again, trying to make out her features more clearly. I tried to guess her age; probably in her late twenties. By all standards, Abayor should be in his late 50s or early 60s.

Why would he have to marry a girl young enough to be his daughter? Anyway, why was I being unnecessarily worried about what did not concern me? As the saying goes marriages are made in heaven. Maybe Abayor took his time in marrying late;

marriage is a lottery, if you marry in haste, you may regret at leisure.

I went on eating and Abayor was reliving our escapades on the Campus in the late70s. It was fun in those days; of going to watch films, attending parties and musical shows, strolling round the Campus at night, screaming for no reason and of course burying our heads in our books when the exams were near...

Abayor reminded me of the numerous times when he had told me to cheat on FM and go out with him. It was a suggestion I had rejected vehemently any time he came up with it. I remember the day he said;

"*Yinkus*, if you don't know how to cheat on your guy, I will teach you".

I laughed out loudly because I never knew I needed a tutorial for cheating skills.

"One day, you will catch your tongue with your teeth", I retorted, looking at Abayor as if he came from the woods!

Chapter 3

What Will Be, Will Be...

Banji Madu's birthday party was one in town... The money bags in the society converged there and money was being sprayed as if it was going out of fashion. The celebrant, Banji (BJ) was on the dance floor and there was Naira and Dollar rain from him and his friends. I looked around and saw some of our Great IFE Alumni digging to the old tunes with calculated dancing steps. From where I was seated, I was nodding my head and stamping my feet to those evergreen funky vibes.

"I'm in the mood to dance. Shall we dance?" Abayor whispered to me.

"Are you sure, Abayor? See..., it doesn't really matter to me whether I danced or not. I could just sit here and look at your 'horrible' face for a while." I pushed him away jokingly. Why would I dance with him when his wife was seated before me?

"No. Let's dance. It will help me let off some steam." He winked at me knowingly.

"To let off steam...? You are not serious o, Abayor...! You have a lot of nerve..."! I said and I swiftly looked towards his wife who was busy browsing on her phone.

He followed my eyes in the direction of his wife and smiled into my eyes. "It is alright, Yinkus."

"If the circumstances were different..." I started by saying this, but I was cut short in the middle of my sentence as Abayor deliberately stepped hard on my toes under the table.

"But they are not, *Yinkus mi...*" He blurted out. "...and it is unfair of you to say so. You know, you and I have been very good friends for years and I cannot say because I am married now I would abandon my old friends." He cautioned me lightly and there was this steady challenging look on his face.

"I know we are all grown up in this make believe world but it doesn't change the fact of our lives." I said, trying to sound casual.

"I had a real crush on you at the Campus and I would have loved to be your boyfriend then, or even be an assistant boyfriend but you were not the least interested in me. I was only tagging after you. You had eyes only for that tall slim guy in glasses...I can't remember his name again". He winked at me.

"Are you alright, Abayor? Oh... Just go away!"

"Memory is a funny thing. Looking back, I had a feeling that you were a no-nonsense girl. You really had a lot of nerves in those days, *Yinkus mi.* You trod on places where angels feared to tread. You seemed so brave at that time. I remember we used to call you "*Woman Soldier.*" He emphasized the ill-fitting nickname my friends gave me.

"Enough! Simmer down, Abayor. Why are you saying all these? Okay, let's dance. People are starting to look interested in what we are saying." I said in very low tones.

Suddenly, I felt quite unexpectedly pleased that he was here and that he still remembers the bond in our friendship. A hall so full of couples can be a bit intimidating when you are on your own and a friendly face can make all the difference. Abayor's face was certainly friendly and rather handsome too!

I resigned to his blackmail and told him I would only dance with him for five minutes. He nodded repeatedly like the Agama lizard and shrugged his shoulders. Abayor touched his wife's hand with a kind of telepathy of telling her he was going away from the table; and she in turn nodded her consent.

"Shall we go?" Abayor whispered into my ears, taking me by the hand.

I nodded silently. He was the first to get up from the table and led the way to the dance floor. We mingled with people and I soon forgot my time target of five minutes. Just as we danced back and forth to the juju sound, Abayor said something into my ears which I didn't hear very well. So, I tilted forward a little bit to hear him. As I did, I could feel my chest grazing the front of his *agbada* and I retreated. He whispered my name into my ear;

"*Yinkus mi,* what's happening to us? You look very lovely. As a Grandma that you are, you are still having this effect on me, just like you did when we were younger on Campus...hmmm."

He said and then looked at me in a way that had my stomach turning to fluid. His eyes were beaming at me as if I was a teenager. I know I should have broken away from him right there and then, or pushed him away, or made an excuse to go and sit down--but I didn't. Yes, I didn't. Just like anyone who is not a stone-hearted saint wouldn't. I think I liked what I was hearing and when I remembered that I was not the young girl of yester-years any longer, I came back to my senses!

"Oh, shut up, will you? Naughty boy! Stop looking at me like that! You are making me feel very uneasy!"

Flashes of the times we were on Campus came to my mind's eye. Those were the days when Abayor and I would dance non-stop for hours at parties. We had a tremendous amount of fun; for the thrill of it, anyway.

Abayor smiled very slowly. "In what way am I making you feel uneasy?" His gaze was so intense. "It would be nice if you'd be a bit more specific about exactly why you are uneasy."

"Next to dancing, interrogation is another thing you are good at." I found myself saying, trying to shift the question."Abayor, say the truth...! I don't understand this amusement in your eyes. Why did you bring me here? Hmm...? To flirt with me or to dance...?"

He said he brought me out to the dance floor to spray me money. As if by mutual signal, BJ the celebrant also moved closer to where we were and threw back his head and laughed heartily;

"Are you enjoying yourselves...? Oh...! I can see that myself"!

I nodded vigorously, digging the dance. He brought out wads of cash and joined Abayor in the money spraying spree! My clutch bag was full of money to the brim.

Later, many of us on the dance floor formed a semi-circle round BJ and his wife and we danced and danced round them. The Band Stand dished out so many old tunes in which we sang along happily, remembering those good old days! There was so much fun!

After a long while, we returned to our table; it was a bit deserted by now as many of the guests had gone to dance. Abayor took permission from his wife to sit beside me. He had not changed much except for the grey beard and the glasses he put on. His voice was still the same; husky in an attractive way. The dimples on his cheeks were still very deep and it made his face to light up any time he smiled. His white set of teeth...hmmm...!

****

Abayor was a very good friend of mine, ever since we were students in the University. He was living in one of the Boys' Quarters at the Staff Quarters. He studied Metallurgical Engineering and was good at it. He told me he had a business outfit of his own. I could see that he had done well for himself by his looks. He looked wealthy and polished.

"You look good in this native attire." I complimented his dressing. "I have never seen you in anything but shirt and jeans trousers or a business suit." I said.

"Oh... Really...?" Abayor roared in laughter. "What about my Birth-day suit?"

"Your Birth-day suit...? What is that?" I asked.

"Yes... That is the suit I came into the world with. My total nakedness! You haven't seen me in that either." He said jokingly in his characteristic humor and candor and then concluded with a wink and a taunting smile.

All I could exclaim with my eyes wide opened was; "Hah? Abayor...!" He ignored my glance and started laughing. Hey...? I looked fugitively around us to be sure no one heard his weird remarks. I made a face as if I was offended and I quickly changed the topic and directed the flashlight of questions at him instead.

"Abayor, I learnt you got married in the middle of the 80s. What happened to her? Your wife I mean."

He broke off with a sharp intake of breath and patted my hands. He said it was a long story and this party was not an ideal place for such intimate talks. He dipped his hand inside his pocket and fished out his purse. He scribbled his home address behind his business card before handing it over to me.

He wanted me to visit them in their house on any weekend if possible. He then showed me the photograph of two young boys of about four years old smiling innocently at the camera. They looked so cute and smart.

"Are these your kids?" I asked.

I took the picture from him and keenly peered closely at the photograph of the identical boys. They were the splitting image of Abayor; and I told him so.

"These are my twins", he said. "They are...my Princes; my joy and the glory of God in my life!"

Abayor's face lit up brightly when he was introducing them, just as he did in a peculiar way when he was introducing their Mum to me earlier on. They must be very special to him.

"Are they your only children?" I had to ask.

"Yes they are! They are my only children."

"Oh? I see!" I reacted.

"*Yinkus mi,* please come over to my house one of these days; preferably this weekend. I want to share my testimony with you." Abayor beamed.

On that note, we closed the chapter of reminiscences of our youthful years on UNIFE Campus; we concentrated on enjoying the party.

An old song of Doris Day**; "Que Sera Sera" (1948)** waltzed across my mind and I could not help doting on the lyrics of the song:

"When I was just a little girl

I asked my mother, "What will I be?

Will I be pretty? Will I be rich..."?

Chapter 4

A Distant Memory

Saturday was like a very long time to come. My ears were itching to hear what Abayor had to say about his life expedition. I wanted to know why Mary-Anne left him and also about the woman he eventually married before this younger woman came into the picture. I was laughing at myself for looking forward to hearing a juicy gist from Abayor; he was good at dishing out gist when we were on Campus.

Whenever anyone was having a Room Birthday party or there was a Social Hall Week, or any social activity on Campus and they needed the services of a comedy compère or a Master of Ceremony, Abayor was the guy to hire for a small token fee. He knew the Campus from stem to stem and we named him the Gist merchant. He wasn't one to joke with his remuneration though. If his full payment was not paid, he would not shift an inch to perform at the show. And because he was good, he was considered to be a hot cake compère. I remember his slogan was, "No quid...No Show!"

I used to wonder why Abayor was so much into money until he told me one day that;

"*Yinkus mi*, you don't understand... Money is like the gasoline that makes my engine to move. It is like the oxygen to sustain me on this Campus. I am not a charity organization. I've got bills to pay, okay?"

It baffled me why he opted to be in the sciences when actually he should have read Theatre Arts or any of those courses in the Humanities. Many of us that were his friends were all in the Arts and he was the odd one out. He was always at the African Studies Pit Theatre or at the bush behind the *Old Buka*, among the Keggites; the Palm wine Drinkers' Club. He was actually their Drumito... meaning, he was the drummer.

So you can imagine my excitement when Abayor invited me over to his house to get the full gist that must be waiting in the cooler to be told. Good a thing, my knowledge in Broadcasting would come in handy when it comes to digging out information from him.

At the dot of 1pm, I drove to Abayor's house and knocked. It was the wife that opened the door; such a pretty lady! She flashed her white set of teeth and knelt down to greet me. I greeted her warmly too;

"How are you my darling? Is your husband indoors?"

"Yes Ma'am."

She stepped aside to make way for me to pass and led the way to the living room. Abayor was there working on his laptop. He raised his head up and beamed at me. He stood up and gave me a bear hug with a hello peck on my cheek. To be candid, it was just a good-to-see-you thing, a polite gesture between old friends. No lips on lips, no tongues, no fireworks. But it didn't stop the little flutter starting up inside me again, just as it had every time I'd looked at him all those years ago when we were at school.

"*Yinkus Babe...* You made it; *beeni tie ri...* I trust you! Thanks for coming. How are you doing?"

"I'm good. We bless God!" I replied.

I looked around and I complimented the nice interior decoration of his house; everything smelt of wealth. The beautiful chandelier that was hung at the center of the living room must have cost a fortune. The place was very neat and tidy.

Looking at the gleaming granite and steel surfaces and the exquisite marble floors, I knew that Abayor had far too much money for his own good. He had stuck a gold-mine too just as BJ had done. The atmosphere in his house was homely and relaxed.

He pointed to a seat for me. His wife had brought a tray of freshly juiced fruits and I nodded my thanks. I was just taking a sip when two adorable boys ran into the living room laughing happily; they chased each other around the center table. At that instant, I knew they were playing a game of *catcher-catcher.* Their Dad called them to order and ordered them to greet me.

Immediately, they stopped being silly and moved closer to me and prostrated flat on the floor. I was very impressed. Such little kids and so respectful...!

"Good afternoon, Ma!" They both chorused in their baby high pitched voices.

They looked so innocent and lovely. I hugged them one after the other and asked of their names; they are Oluwatise Taiwo Durogbajo and Iyanuoluwa Kehinde Durogbajo. Such Lovely names...!

They quickly disappeared through the door in which they came and I turned to face their Dad. I told him I was quite impressed by the show his sons put up now. I commended him for training them to know our morals and values from formative years; a case of train up your child the way he should go. When he grows older, he will not depart from it.

"Oh Yes...I am a firm believer that, if you raise a child in the right way, you will not have to fix an adult." He said.

Half an hour later, we had a sumptuous lunch and were reclining on our seats over some chilled fruit wine. We were watching a certain Documentary on the TV when Abayor suddenly looked at me and busted into laughter. I looked towards him with an enquiring frown on my forehead but he kept on laughing and pointing at me. Abayor loved to tease; I could give him a credit for that...!

"*Yinkus mi...!* If I know you very well, you are dying to ask me questions from this beautiful head of yours. Okay, go ahead and ask anything you wish to know."

Truly, I wanted to ask questions and he had even given me the green light but how would one ask questions when the person involved was seated with us? I didn't say a word; I just smiled and sipped my drink. From the rim of my glass of fruit wine that I held close to my face, I stole a glance at his wife in the room with us and I quickly looked away. Abayor caught my eyes and exclaimed in a high spirited voice.

"*Yinkus, Yinkus...*! I will tell you my story. It is a long story, though. Will you have the patience to listen through it without interruption?"

I smiled and promised him that I would not interrupt. Once more, I took a sip from my wine and darted a glance at his wife yet again. As if on cue, Abayor's wife stood up and excused herself saying she had things to do upstairs. She left with her children. It couldn't have been a better time to take her exit because I would not have been able to concentrate if she was seated there with us. I was relieved to see her leave the living room.

The coast was cleared now. I sat uprightly and spoke in a low voice, asking Abayor what happened to his Campus beau, Mary-Anne? He told me to relax and speak normally. He said his wife was not within earshot. I relaxed my mind and stood up to view the beautiful family portrait that was hung on the wall. I moved to the personal picture of his wife and told him his wife was beautiful.

For an instant, I almost envied her. It is funny how a total stranger can make you look twice at yourself. She set me thinking about my FM; my husband and his ice-cool level-headedness. Gloomily, jealously, I sensed that this lady has experienced some degree of sheer unbridled happiness and I couldn't but wonder why Abayor chose to marry such a very young girl. Well, it was none of my business really, but I just couldn't help myself thinking about it.

As I went back to sit down, Abayor smiled and said he was lucky to have married his present wife. Within me, I said it means there was a wife before or even wives before this present one. Anyway, a vulture is a patient bird. I decided not to put the cart before the horse. I would wait patiently and listen to his juicy gist.

Abayor flashed me his white set of teeth. Actually, those teeth were part of why I liked him when we were in the University. I remember the time I wanted to ask him what type of toothpaste he was using but I couldn’t bring myself to ask. You know, in those days of my generation, girls were not to first show affection to a guy openly. It was not in vogue to be the first to tell a guy you liked him.

So, as I was saying, Abayor had asked me if I could be patient enough to listen to his story without interrupting. Hmmm...! Knowing the kind of nature God has blessed me with, would I be able to sit straight and listen without putting a word? Anyway, I told Abayor to shoot! But he said;

"*Yinkus mi*... I am going to start this story from the beginning so that you'd understand where I am coming from and how I found myself married to a woman that is young enough to be my daughter." He said solemnly with a faint smile and with that air of something left unsaid.

I nodded and stole a glance at the hung personal portrait of the woman again who was smiling lovingly at me. My eyes darted back to Abayor and I kept my mouth shut because that was our agreement if he was to open the windows of his life for me to peep.

"Do you know that, with the exception of my wife, I have never told my whole story to anyone before now? I have only told it in bits to my friends when I was in the secondary school. I consent to people who wish to speculate anything they wish to say and form their opinions. I am sure they have gossiped and said all sorts of stuff behind my back, but I couldn't be bothered. I have grown a thick skin over the years."

He said as he shrugged his shoulders and stretched his legs lazily before continuing what he was saying;

"Why am I even telling you this...*Yinkus mi*?" He looked at me and grimaced. "I don't know... Maybe for old time sake or maybe it is time to reveal what I have bottled up in my heart for years. None of my siblings wanted to listen to my story in those years of vulnerability. Any time I tried to voice it out, they would shush me down. They were so afraid of our eldest brother and didn't want to offend him. I believe the time is ripe for me to tell my story to the world and allow them to judge me. I suffered a great deal of self reproach and I suffered from insomnia too. I am a man who survived horrible psychological abuse and harassment; a man who has navigated through the system and survived. I am that man standing; the one who no one could turn into a dwarf. I am God's template of the miraculous! I had gone to hell and back! Today, it seems like a distant memory."

SONGS OF PRAISE

Father, I place into your hands

The troubles of my life

Father, I place into your hands

The pains I have been through

Father, I place into your hands

The story of my life ...

For I know I always can trust you!

Chapter 5

The Bully

Abayomi kept mute for what seemed like ages. He was staring at the wall as if the story he wanted to tell me was being scrolled on the wall and he was searching for which button to press. I was tempted to say he should go on talking or maybe I should tap him back to reality but I had a better judgment to wait for him.

I sat still, not moving an inch; trying not to disrupt his line of thoughts. Maybe he was trying to change his mind about revealing his story to me. I prayed a silent prayer against such evil thoughts. *Today na today...!*

After what seemed like many minutes, he removed his eyes from the wall and looked at me dejectedly. I panicked a little bit, thinking he was going to apologize and change his mind. Instead, he shook his head and said;

"*Yinkus mi,* I don't seem to know where to start. Everything is rushing back at me like a speeding train. I am confused as it is. I really don't know...."

I told him to start from the beginning. After all, the beginning of a long journey starts from the first step. He nodded and cleared his throat loudly. He again warned me not to say a single word until he was done with his story. I quickly held my lips tightly with my fingers to indicate perfect silence, like the kindergarten kids would do to assure their teacher they were in perfect silence.

He sipped his drink and gazed into space as the horrific event flooded back. He remembered it all. For the umpteenth time, Abayor sighed.

"Okay, *Yinkus mi...* I will do a playback of my life. I will tell you the story of my life from the beginning as I remember it. My name, as you know, is Abayomi Oriyomi Durogbajo. I am the last child of my parents in the family of nine children; seven males and two females. From my names, you would have guessed that a story was attached to them.

ABAYOMI-- *means people could have scorned me if not for the mercy of God.*

ORIYOMI-- *means I experienced divine intervention.*

I didn't bother about the meaning of those names initially while my parents were alive; until their death when my eldest brother scorned me to death and reiterated that I was an unwanted child. He said my parents were not my real parents and that I was adopted. How I cried that day! Anyway, don't let me jump the gun. I will come back to that part of the story later on.

As I was saying, these are my names. My parents had a fatal car crash that claimed both lives. They were in transit to the Eastern part of the country to see an old friend of theirs in Nsukka when the ill fated tragic accident happened.

Their death threw a bad spanner into the fire because the last three of us in the family were still young and vulnerable. I was the hardest hit because I was the last child of nine children.

Looking back at how I survived the sibling rivalry still amazes me till date. I had to do the meanest chores because I was the last child. I got sent on errands that no one else was willing to do. I only got a time of respite at night when everyone had slept. Everything would start and end on top of my head, there was always fights and commotions in the house. You would hear;

"Who dropped this glass on the floor?" Someone would ask. And as he was asking, another person would shout from another angle;

"It must be Abayor, no doubt. Very clumsy boy"!

Meanwhile, I would scream from where ever I was that I wasn't the culprit. The oldest of my brothers (I nicknamed him Big Brother), would not even find out who actually did wrong before he would sit in judgment and pronounced me guilty. I was always severely punished by him for another person's wrong doings. Most of the time, the culprit would sneak from behind to beg me for forgiveness as I wouldn't stop crying. You know how agonizing it could be when you are being punished unjustly.

My eldest brother's name is Diekola. While we were all growing up, he was the bully that no one wanted as a brother. He could beat any of us to stupor and would be praising himself for a job well done.

Anytime my path crossed his own along the corridor or anywhere in the house, he would stop to look at me with disdain and pretend to spit me from his mouth. His volcanic anger was fierce! No one steps on his toes and expects to be spared.

Meanwhile, my heart would be doing its beats in multiple somersaults because I would not be able to tell if he was going to give me double slaps or a knock on the head. I used to walk with trepidation near him. I regarded him as the "He" that must be feared and obeyed!

My mother had warned Big Brother several times to adjust his behavior in interacting with his siblings but he had turned a deaf ear to her pleas. On many occasions he would talk back at our parents and would walk out on them. All these atrocities, we the younger ones were watching.

There was a time our mother was very ill and needed to take her medication. She was too weak to stand up from the bed, so she called her eldest son for assistance;

"Diekola, could you please make a little pap for me? I wish to take my drugs now." Mother said in a very low tone.

"Oh oooo...! Not again! Which pap? I can't be making any pap now... Must I not rest again?"Big Brother stamped his feet on the ground several times to depict his annoyance at being sent on an errand.

My Mother heaved a deep sorrowful sigh and slowly sat up from her sick bed. She faced Big Brother and told him again to go and make the pap. He hissed and left the room. Mother waited for almost an hour but Big Brother did not show up. I was therefore asked to check on him in the kitchen; he was not there. I checked his room and everywhere else, he was not there. He must have left the house in anger.

So, I went back to tell Mother my findings. She was pained to the bone marrow. That was not the first time her eldest son would cause her sorrow. She was so weak and frail. She needed to take her medication and she must eat before doing that.

However, she called one of my other brothers-- Brother Solomon who was a few years younger than Big Brother to make that pap for her. She then explained to him how the pap would be made.

Long after mother had eaten and taken her medication, Big Brother strolled in from wherever he went. I ran to tell Mother and I got the hell of a beating for that singular act from the bully of our family. My Mother was too weak to scold him and the situation was getting worse by the day. He was so brutal to me that I dreaded hearing his voice in the house.

"Diekola...! You have turned yourself to a terror in this family! Leave my child alone!"

That was how Mother used to shout any time the devil in the heart of our Big Brother roared that he turned me to his punching bag.

****

The day Big Brother got his appointment letter to be a Grade 2 Teacher in a Primary School in Osogbo, was a joyous day for all of us in the family. We were kind of saying with our body language that it was "good riddance to bad rubbish."

We all rejoiced at the news that our most feared terrorist was leaving us to start a new life of his own. We did not rejoice in his presence anyway! Who would dare do it? "*Who born monkey...*"?

Early in the morning of his departure, he became unnecessarily nice to me; telling me to take care of myself and be a good boy. I couldn't wait to see his back. I was counting the minutes; nothing should delay his going away; unfortunately, there was a little wait.

It was Deoye -- one of my brothers who gave a valedictory speech in front of the house, saying nice things about Big Brother. He said that we would all miss him for being a responsible, caring and dutiful big brother to all of us.

We all remained quiet, listening to a bunch of lies that Deoye was spewing out. Big Brother Diekola was in deep thoughts. We could depict this from the criss-cross pattern of lines on his forehead. He was probably thinking whether to believe Deoye or not, but he looked sober!

The vehicle to take him to Osogbo parked in front of the house and we all helped him to load his luggage. He sat beside the driver and was waving sorrowfully as if he was sad to leave us. Meanwhile, I was excited and relieved to see him go.

Eventually, the bus driver roared his engine and sped off. We waited outside watching the tail of the car. As soon as the vehicle was out sight, we descended on Deoye who gave the "valedictory speech" and demanded to know why he told such a big lie.

"I didn't mean it. I wanted him to have a nice feeling that his siblings loved him so much," Deoye said as he tried to defend himself. "All the things I said were only from my lips and not from my heart."

"What if he decides to change his mind and come back home?" Our Father asked and before he could finish asking we all chorused a loud "God forbid!"

It was a nice relief that the bully of the family had left. We couldn't have been much happier. No one mentioned his name and we all pretended he was never part of our family. I have to tell you that the happiness was punctured barely six months that Big Brother left home.

Our parents died in a fatal road crash. They were on their way to Nsukka to visit my Father's bosom friend, Prof Emeka Ozigwu. Father had asked Mother to come with him for company. We never knew we were waving the final bye-bye when on that fateful Saturday that my parents set out on the journey of no return.

We, the younger children in the house became like the sheep without a shepherd. Our older siblings were in various Universities while we, the younger ones were in the secondary school. We were wondering what would happen to us as our parents had died. Many people from far and near came to console us.

Big Brother Diekola came home for the burial and he wept profusely. I remember wondering why he was crying so much when all the while our parents were alive he gave them so much heartache and misery. Everyone who knew his real nature was shocked to see him cry.

While our parents were alive, there was no one he could not abuse or be rude to. There is no civil tongue in his head. My mother's siblings also got the acidic side of his tongue and thereafter they conversed with him in great trepidation.

****

Funeral rites were over and everyone went to their homes. Several family meetings were held and a communiqué was issued. Big Brother put his foot down that he would take me along with him to his station in Osogbo to start a new life there. I busted into hot tears when the reality dawn on me that I would be his responsibility thereafter.

I searched the faces of my other siblings why they would allow such evil to befall me. They avoided my eyes as they had no say in this matter. No one bothered about my feelings but because our Big Brother had spoken, his commands had to be obeyed. Truly, destiny has a wicked sense of humor!

I didn't fancy the idea of going to live in Osogbo at all because this Big Brother and I were never on good terms; he never saw anything good in what I did. Now that the verdict had been given, I couldn't resist or revolt. There was no one to rescue me from his claws. He was the *Daodu,* the first son! He held all the aces of the family's cards. He held the joker too!

"*Pele*.... Abayor. Don't worry; we would all be visiting you in Osogbo from time to time", Brother Bola said quietly while consoling me. He was moved to tears himself. I was in Form one then, in the secondary school. Brother Adebola (Bola for short) is the next son to Big Brother Diekola.

Okay, let me mention our names. This is how we stand in the family.

(i)Big Brother Diekola,

(ii)Brother Bola,

(iii)Brother Gabriel,

(iv)Brother Solomon,

(v)Sister Tundun,

(vi)Sister Laide,

(vii)Wale,

(viii)Deoye and my humble self,

(ix) Abayomi.

I cried so much as I was being led to the vehicle that would take us to Osogbo. I looked back at our house and remembered my mother. If not for her death, what would have made me to be the one chosen to live with Big Brother when I knew he hated me with passion?

Yinkus mi, are you listening to my story? Okay. It is so difficult to put into words my feelings as I was being led to the Osogbo bound vehicle. I felt like a dog being kept on a leash and being led out. I looked helplessly about me; I was leaving the comfort of my home, my school, my friends and neighborhood.

The torrential tears would not stop. Just as I was being reluctant to go, Big Brother grabbed my arm and hustled me into the waiting vehicle. The city of Osogbo became my new home thereafter!

Chapter 6

Weapons of Punishment

My journey to Hell began the very day I stepped into Big Brother's house in Osogbo. He sat me down and gave me the draconian laws of his house; the dos and don'ts of my conduct. I listened carefully and I decided to keep to my lane if I didn't want his trouble.

Despite the fact that I kept away from Big Brother, he didn't let me be. My presence in his house irritated him so much that he always had this murderous look on his face anytime I bumped into him in the house and he would bark orders at me. In other words, he turned me into his slave in his house; a glorified domestic servant, so to speak.

That was how I found myself in the den of a fierce lion in human being's clothing; maybe I should call it Slavery Shelter House. I was badly used, psychologically abused and humiliated in Big Brother Diekola's house every minute of the day. It was as if I had offended him in his previous life and he had made up his mind to have his pound of flesh on me. It was a tyrannical rule.

Firstly, he reduced my psyche to a boy of no value. He constantly told me each morning that I meant nothing to the family and I would amount to nothing in the nearest future. Day after day, I would weep profusely before going out to face the world. He was so hostile to me that I often wondered what I did to deserve such treatment. I was always in a permanent state of mourning. No day passed without my thoughts on my late Mum.

I had to withdraw into my shell as I didn't know how else to behave; I was totally disorientated. He would yell at me for no reason and say I had wronged him, even though he refused to tell me what I had done wrong.

All my friends could not visit or talk freely with me. I had to stop them from writing letters to me because Big Brother would read the letters and used the content to mock me on how useless I had become to receive letters from Pen Pals. He was always snooping about in my leather box looking for exhibits to nail me.

"Please Sir; tell me my offence so that I would know how to correct myself." I always pleaded with him.

I lived in terror of Big Brother and I had to plead with him to stop this act of intimidation; instead, he would scream and say I was planning to kill him. He unleashed on me daily, great venom of hatred. This was so confusing to me. What did I do wrong to warrant such monumental hatred?

I was always walking on eggshells within the house, trying not to upset him; yet I never had a minute of respite. I was always doing house chores. He hated seeing me by my books. If he saw that I was reading, he would call me away from it and send me to wash, clean, tidy and mop everything in the house.

My school days in Big Brother's house were hellish. There was a day I was preparing for a class assessment, so I sat at my books studying. He peeped from the door and saw me reading and exclaimed;

"Abayomi...! These walls are dirty! Leave whatever you are doing and wash all the walls of this house. I must not see any fingerprint on them again."

"...To wash the wall"? I told him solemnly that I was preparing for an assessment test and I would wash the walls later. Haaa! *Yinkus mi...* You needed to see how he flared up that day. His shriek shouts hit me like a tidal waves. He descended on me with blows and kicks for defying his orders. I have so many tell tale marks of his beatings on my body.

He would curse me and would tell me to my face that I was an unwanted child of our parents. The day he first said this, I cried so much because I believed he was saying the truth. He told me to ask around from our Aunties and Uncles and verify the story. I did, but they all told me it was not true.

Big Brother would invite all his Teacher colleagues living within the same school Quarters to his house and would tell them how useless and worthless I was. I became their topic of discussion anytime they got together. Those friends too would add insult to my injury and fabricate false stories about me just to gain a point in their gathering. You would hear them say;

"Oh, I saw Abayor along the road to *Alekuwodo* this evening. He was talking with a girl in a compromising position."

Another one would say, "I saw him waving at a girl this morning..."

For each of the accusations they fabricated, I got the beating of my life as if the world was coming to an end. Coming home from school was a dilemma. I hated it when it was closing time to go home.

All other students would jubilate at the jingle sound of the bell to end school hours, but I, Abayomi Durogbajo would be near tears. I knew what trouble was awaiting me in Big Brother's house. I had no money of my own.

This was the bitterest pill for me to swallow in all the years I had lived with Big Brother. Money, or should I say the lack of it was the weapon he used to curb me. He made sure I had no money at hand at any moment and he would discourage anyone that wanted to give me. If I was given any cash by any visitor in his presence, he would collect it from me after the visitor might have gone. He would say;

"Do you know what they use money for? Tell me....! Do you know? You are such a useless fellow that you can never know the value of money. Hand it over to me now! Stupid boy... Tall for nothing! Shiooor"!

He would then snatch the money from my hand with a loud hiss! Or he would give me a knock on my head. I cannot begin to tell you the number of knocks my head had received from him over the years.

Anyway, that was in the early days when I didn't know that it was not wise to stand so close to him. His knuckles were always itching for something to knock; my poor head was the unfortunate prey. Later, when I knew the tricks, I would stand at a distance and say whatever I wanted to say to him.

Food was another weapon used to punish me. I was really deprived of food in that house. Big Brother felt that eating a three square meal was a luxury. He devised a way of making sure I ate once a day. I was not to eat breakfast to school even though I was going to trek all the way of about 15 kilometers.

I always got back home around 4pm, if there was no extra lesson in school; but if there was an afternoon lesson, I would get home by 6pm to prepare the evening meal.

By the time I was done with cooking, it would have been 8pm, or much earlier if the food I was to prepare was simple and plain. Even though I was the one who prepared the food, I was always given a little portion of it to eat. That was to be my only meal for the day.

My school was a very far distance to where we lived, yet I was expected to trek to school and back. Initially, I was always late and I got punished severely for it in school; but as time went on, I devised a plan to wake up earlier than usual. I made a plan to wake up by 4.30am. I had clothes to wash, food to prepare and the house to sweep and mop. All these chores had to be done before stepping out of the house by 6am.

The first time I devised a plan to wake up early was a day to remember. Let me tell you the story. I woke up by 3.30am by mistake instead of 4.30am. I rushed at what I had to do...sweeping and mopping the floor, washing clothes, cooking and tiding the house. I did all these hurriedly and left the house.

I was not aware that the time was 4.35am. As I stepped out of the house, the whole neighborhood was eerie sort of. The atmospheric noise of an early morning was not there; no sound of a living being was heard; only my footsteps. I could only hear the sounds of birds making *shio shio* sounds from a distance.

I got to a junction with three pathways at the heart of the city and all of a sudden, I felt very frightened and it gave me goose pimples; it was as if my head had swollen to double its original size. I felt I was not alone on the street even though no one else was with me physically. I imagined some scary goblins were watching me. I looked around and I quickened my footsteps; I was taking long strides and walking briskly. My heart began to beat like a basket-ball being dribbled down a fast court. It was sounding hard and loud like this-*gbi...gbaga...gbi...gbaga*!

I kept on looking back to be sure no one was following me. Suddenly I heard someone sneezed loudly from a dilapidated kiosk. I turned to look and I nearly jumped out of my skin for fright. It was a deranged man!

"Hey! Who goes there? Come back here..."!

He snarled at me and stood up like a flash. He jumped the gutter in front of him and made to chase after me. Without wasting time, I turned to a sprinter and ran like crazy. You know, I ran like the world acclaimed sprinter, Usain Bolt would run with the wind... I mean Usain Bolt, the fastest Olympic runner of his time.

I could hear from a distance, the deranged man's footsteps behind me as I ran blindly early that morning. I didn't make attempt to turn back to look; I was using the sound of his footsteps to judge the distance of the gap between us. After a while, I couldn't hear anything again but the sound of my footsteps only. That was when I slowed down and turned. I was still running but not as furious as when the man was pursuing me.

Later, I stopped running and I was panting heavily. I felt like sitting down to rest but I dared not try it. So I stooped down with my hands on my two knees and rested for a while but I was on the watch of that mad man or any other crazy fellow lurking around. I must have covered quite a long distance while running.

When I eventually got to *Olaiya* Street, I realized that the early risers who usually sell hot drinks for motorists were not there and also the newspaper vendors. At that point, I knew something was amiss. I must have checked the time wrongly at home. There was no way to know what the time was. I made a mental reminder to tell Brother Bola, my other brother to buy wrist watch for me at his next visit.

I got to school safe and sound. The Gateman was shocked to see me. He pointed his touch to my face and asked where I was coming from.

"Where are you coming from at this time of the day? I am sure you didn't sleep at home."

He directed the touch to his wrist watch to check the time. The beam of his touch also scrutinized me from head to toe. I looked tired, disheveled and pale. I was drenched in my sweat and panting not too heavily this time around. He asked again where I was coming from and I gave him blow by blow narration of my encounter with the deranged man.

He then asked if I had a mother and how could she have allowed me to leave the house so early at the crack of dawn. I told him my parents were dead and I lived with someone who hated me. He sympathized a little and I quickly asked if I could pass through the gate. I didn't want any more interrogation.

I got to school when the School Boarders were waking up. I was just climbing the staircase to my class when I heard the 1st wake-up bell for the seniors from afar; the time must have been 5.30am. Wow! I decided to rest and take a nap before the start of the day! I pulled many chairs together to make a bed and slept like a baby!

I didn't know for how long I had slept, but from my dream world, I heard the voices of the other students at the school Hall assembly reciting the **Angelus**;

"Hail Mary full of grace

The Lord is with thee

Blessed art thou amongst women

And blessed is the fruit of thy womb Jesus.

Holy Mary, Mother of God

Pray for us sinners, now

And at the hour of our death, Amen"!

In the name of the Father

And of the Son

And of the Holy Spirit, Amen.

Chapter 7

In the Depth of Despair

As I look back now in retrospect, I remember the days I would cry myself to sleep. There was no day I did not remember my late mother and I would plead with God to make me die and join my parents. Hmm ... I was so depressed in those days that I wanted to put an end to my life. Yes...!

Thoughts of suicide crept into my mind a number of times and I had attempted ending it all each time but I kept bouncing back alive by divine intervention. Big Brother added to my depression by always telling me to go and die as no one wanted me alive;

"What is your usefulness in this family"? He snarled at me one day. "No one wants you around; you are just occupying space for nothing. Don't you know you have a horrible destiny? Go and die!"

To me, suicide was not just an ugly word; it was a real option. It was a decision I made almost on daily basis. I thought it would be an easy way out to end the torment for me. I really wanted to die! Truth needs to be told, *Yinka mi.* I nearly had a psychological disorder. I was depressed and I didn't know who I was anymore.

I realized that I used to hear echoes of Big Brother's curses and abuses in my head. The oozing noise made me to have throbbing headache at all times. This made me turn to pain killer drugs for succor and at every point of the thump; I would take a double dose of the pain killers. After then, I would go for a very long walk and trekked with no determinant destination. While I walked, the noise throbbed and I seemed to hear instructions in Big Brother's voice;

"Just go and die! No one wants you here... You are only an unwanted child; a good for nothing fool... You cannot make it in life... How could you make it, when it is not two for a penny...? What is your usefulness in this life?"

I used to hear all these abuses re-echoing in my head as I walked to get fresh air. The only thing I wanted to do at such times was to just end my life there and then. I was in and out of depression bout.

There was a day I left the house and I wandered aimlessly along the busy streets of Osogbo. I had no definite destination in mind, but I needed to get fresh air because I was being suffocated with curses and abuses at home.

However, I didn't realize that I was talking aloud to myself. In my sub-conscious mind, I knew people were staring at me but I was lost to the world. I trekked so far from home and I got to an intersection junction. I crossed the road without looking out for traffic.

I did not realize a car was coming at a top speed at the time I was crossing the road. I moved so slowly like a zombie with no feelings. The people around screamed and wailed so loudly. The driver of the car screeched to a halt just in front of me; I was still in the middle of the road talking to myself and walking so slowly with tears streaming down my face. How the car did not crush me remained a misery to the onlookers!

I remember I looked sideways to see the car very near me. I looked away and continued to walk on. The driver was saying something that my ears couldn't pick. The people were saying all sorts of things but it seemed as if I was hearing them from afar... I mean I heard them faintly in my sub consciousness. I heard them saying;

"Oh ...What a pity..! This boy is a fresh mentally deranged person; he has not yet "*entered the market*". Eeeyah! He looks all right but he must be depressed about something...."!

It was one elderly woman who moved closer to me and held my hand. I stopped to look at her and I tried to withdraw my hand but her grip was firmer. She didn't say anything but kept on walking with me until we got to one *Buka,* a Local Restaurant along the road. We entered and sat down. The woman ordered for three wraps of *amala,* yam flour paste, okro soup and two pieces of meat. She shoved the plate of food before me and told me to eat. I made an attempt to object but she would not hear of it.

I ate the whole food and I was so full and contented. I could not remember the last time I ate so much food. I looked at the woman and I thanked her profusely. She told me she packed her car beside the road where she met me. She saw the way I crossed the road and knew I could not have been a mad person. She was convinced that I was depressed about something and that I might be scared to enter her car, which was why we trekked to the Restaurant.

She asked if I wanted to share my thoughts with her and I said no. I never wanted strangers to know what I was going through because there was nothing they could do about it. The woman gave me so much money and also gave me the description of her shop down town. She wanted me to come around any time I felt like.

To tell you the truth, that was the last time I saw her. I didn't go to her shop for fear of meeting Big Brother's friends. They might see me there and report to him. That would be another round of serious beating in the house.

A profound incident happened to me one day that turned the hand of the clock of suicide in my life. I had boarded a vehicle going to Ibadan and I had made up my mind to kill myself on the way. Listen to how it started...

The morning of that day came as any other morning, Big Brother was angry at me as usual for whatever he thought I had done wrong. He was always claiming I had offended him but he refused to tell me my offense. I prostrated flat on the floor and held his two legs in supplication. I begged him in tears, imploring him to let me know what exactly made him to be so cruel to me.

He raised his legs up and landed them on my head. I screamed and held my head as I cried out so loudly and was weeping profusely. He began to rain curses on me as usual as it was his practice.

He launched into a tirade of abuse against me. All sorts of negative words were coming from his mouth. He told me to get out of his sight, I refused. He stood up and ordered me out of the room; I remained standing and was crying. He roared angrily and moved to the dining table.

Big Brother grabbed a tin of milk and threw it at me in anger. Immediately, I saw splashes of stars in many different colors in my eye. The content of the tin was full, so its impact on my eye was fatal. The sharp edge of the tin had grazed the tip of my left eye-lid. I screamed again in pain as I used my left hand to cover my eye;

"Yee...! My eyes ooo! Haa ...! I am in trouble... ooo!"

I realized that the left hand I used in covering my eye was wet, so I removed it and saw blood dripping from my hand. I panicked! I thought for a minute that I had gone blind, I cried louder than I did before;

"Somebody help me, please oo...Yeee...! Look at blood... I am in trouble ooo....Haaa...I am blind ooo..."!

I rushed to the bathroom to wash my face. I could not open the eye because of the pain. I didn't know what type of First Aid to apply; I was just pouring water on it to rinse the blood. Eventually, the blood flow stopped. I came to the living room but Big Brother had left the house.

I sat down dejectedly, thinking about my life. I thought about my late parents; my mother in particular; my bleak future, because I could see nothing good in it. I remembered how Big Brother used to say that I didn't have any usefulness in the family; how he had told me a countless of time to go and die; that he was tired of seeing my face. He actually wanted me dead!

Everything was rushing back to me; the insults, the curses, the abuses, the humiliation, the beatings, the food starvation, the stress of trekking each day to school on empty stomach; my other brothers who were passive and were unable to stand for me and challenge our Big Brother. I remembered the time he had threatened to make me go dumb when I challenged him of being too harsh on me. He had spitted on me with all venom. When it comes to conflict, Big Brother is a veteran! Hear what he said; "If you ever talk like that to me again, I will slap you to the extent that you will speak in gestures for the rest of your life."

I was wise to know that it wasn't a flimsy threat and that he could do as he had said. To my injured eye; I didn't know whether I was partially or completely blind. Big Brother didn't bother to find out about the condition of the eye before storming out. I still have the scar till today; I have the terror in my heart and the memory in my mind.

I would have been blind, if not for the mercy of God! A memory that won't be banished, it will never go away. I was overwhelmed by all these happenings. The only solution was to do the inevitable! Yes, it would be over today! Death, wait for me! I exclaimed!

My left eye was already swollen as if I had conjunctivitis *(Apollo).* I took the little money I had on me and left the house. At the motor park, I boarded a vehicle going to Ibadan. It was a Peugeot car of six passengers and the ride was smooth. After traveling for several kilometers along Ife/Ibadan expressway, we got to a certain flowing Dam along the route; I told the driver I had reached my stop.

"I am getting down here, Sir." I called out solemnly.

"Where...? Do you want to ease yourself"? The driver asked in an impatient tone. He went on to say he disliked it when passengers stopped to ease themselves while in transit.

"I am not stopping you for the fun of it. I have reached my destination". I barely spew out the words in low tones.

Everyone in the car let out a whistle sigh and they looked around the bush as if they were seeing it for the first time. They could not understand why anyone would claim this bridge with a dam was their destination. A woman sitting at the back seat asked if I was sure it was where I was going. I said yes. I told the man sitting by the door to allow me to come down. He did and I alighted from the vehicle without looking back.

I moved towards the railings of the bridge as I heard the sound of the car leaving. I stood at the railings and said a silent prayer to God to forgive me for what I was about to do. Like a flash and within minutes too, pictures of my parents came before me, I also saw faces of my entire siblings (except Big Brother) one after the other. I knew they would be sad at my death but I couldn't help myself. I said goodbye to them in that trance.

By this time, tears were flowing down my face; I was agonizingly pained in the heart. I just fixed my eyes on the gushing water that was flowing into the dam as I made preparation to jump into it.

All of a sudden, as if I was watching a film, the images of my parents were splayed before me. The apparition was on the gushing water in front of me. I saw my father in a pensive mood. His hands were folded on his chest while he kept shaking his head as if he was rejecting an idea.

My mother was standing beside him. She was distraught and wailing as if she was calling people to help her. Her two hands were flying in the air and intermittently she would grab her head. She was pacing up and down frantically. As I stood there, her voice came to me and I heard what she was saying; "Hah...aaa....! Somebody please help my son... Don't make him come to me yet... Please help my son... Have mercy on him please... Help my son... Help my son... please..."!

I was moved to tears by her pleadings. Who was my Mother calling upon to help me? Why was she sobbing bitterly like this? I stretched my hand towards the dam as if I wanted to calm her down. I called on her in a loud voice;

"*Maami*...! Don't cry...! I am here now! I am coming to you.... Wait for me ..."!

As I said this, I started climbing the railings in preparation to jump into the dam to meet them. Then I heard my father screamed my name hysterically;

"Abayomi.....!!!! Stop..."!

Suddenly, I felt powerful hands gripping each of my shoulders from behind and another one pulled my shirt collar from behind. I was pulled down and I searched their faces to know who they were. The three men that pulled me down were my co-travelers from Osogbo some minutes ago. They didn't utter a single word; they just pulled me down and dragged me between them, away from the dam.

I turned to look at the waterfall to see my parents one more time but I didn't see anything. Everything was just calm; the water was falling down from the height peacefully and I didn't hear the agonizing cry of my mother either.

The three men led me on as if I was a lamb going to be slaughtered; I was trying to free myself from them but their grip was very firm. Minutes later, I looked at a distance and saw a car parked by the roadside. It was the same car that brought me from Osogbo.

All the other occupants were standing by the car watching us and shaking their heads somberly. When we got to them, I realized that they were all very gloomy and troubled. One of the women commended the men who were dragging me;

"Thank goodness, you guys got there on time. Well done Sirs! Ha? What on earth could have depressed this young boy to have planned to end his life? Could he have been under a spell"?

The other woman too added her voice in anger; "Well done, Sirs. Look here, this boy! Are you crazy? What type of rubbish was that...? Eh"?

"Please don't complicate matters for him. He doesn't need all that shouting for now...please"! The elderly man who was among those who came for me at the Dam, reprimanded the two women.

"Please let everybody go into the car and let's leave".

The driver, who had stood by the side of his door watching the goings-on, spoke and shook his head. All of them were looking at me solemnly. We all got in the car. I was squeezed in the middle of two of those men who came for me; the third guy sat in the front seat beside the driver. The car roared into action and we continued our journey.

No one spoke; it was as if nothing happened; everyone with their own thoughts. I could feel the eyes of the two women sitting behind me piercing through my shirt at the back. The older man shut his eyes tightly as if fighting vehemently against the recall of an unpleasant incident. He held my hand closest to him and was humming a familiar Baptist Church **hymnal**;

"Jesus is the entire world to me

My life, my joy, my all;

He is my strength from day to day

Without Him I would fall

When I am sad, to Him I go,

No other one can cheer me so;

When I am sad He makes me glad".

He sang this hymn many times over and then he heaved a deep sigh. He started on the praise eulogy of God Almighty. He was thanking and praising God. Afterwards he parted my hand and asked of my name;

"Young man... what is your name"?

"I am Abayomi Durogbajo, Sir".

"How old are you"?

"I am fifteen years old, Sir".

At the mention of my age, the two elderly women at the back seat, hissed and hissed with so many exclamations...*"eeyah, hoo"!*

"Where are your parents"? The elderly man asked.

"They are dead, Sir". I replied tearfully when I remembered that I saw their apparition a while ago.

"No wonder"! The older man heaved a deep sigh. He went on to tell all of us in the car that he heard the shrieking voice of a woman inside his head urging him tearfully to save her son. That was why he appealed to the driver to reverse the car so as to rescue the young boy that said the river dam was his destination. He said it was a good thing they got there on time as I was about to jump.

Suddenly, the elderly man turned to me sharply. He wanted to know why a young boy of my age would think suicide was the solution to whatever challenge I was facing. As I was about to talk, I was overwhelmed by emotions and I cupped my face into my hands and started crying. I wept for a very long time until I was spent.

I started singing a dirge in a sorrowful tone. It was a sad song and it tugged at the heartstrings of the people in the car. The women hissed again and sighed.

The elderly Baba did not cajole me to stop. He only put his hand across my shoulders and was rocking me. The other man at the other side offered me a clean white handkerchief to clean my face.

It was then pieces of advice started coming from the passengers of that car left, right and center. Everyone had experiences of this world to share with me. I was told it was a grave sin in the sight of God to take one's life. At the end of the day, the elderly *Baba* counseled me so much from the Bible, to the extent that I was rejuvenated.

I was recharged to go back and take up the pieces of my life from where I left it. No more suicide thoughts for me! We finally landed in Ibadan and everyone was about to drop at the motor terminus.

The *Baba* offered to pay my transport fare back to Osogbo. He wanted me to go back home. I said I would rather sleep in Brother Bola's house in Ibadan than return to where I was coming from.

He held my hand and dropped a lump sum of money in my palm. I opened it and saw the money; without minding that I was in the open public, I went flat on the ground and prostrated. I thanked him profusely and I became teary again. The man wiped my tears and encouraged me to be brave like a man!

My left eye that Big Brother wounded had swollen and doubled its size. It was so red and a blood clot was at the eyelid. The Baba took me to a Pharmacy Store where drugs were prescribed and he paid.

He followed me to Brother Bola's house at the UCH Staff Quarters. I told him not to enter the gate as I didn't want questions to be asked by my brother if he saw us.

The old man hugged me as if I was his son and prayed for me. We exchanged contacts and he promised to be checking me up in my school periodically. We said our goodbyes and I went indoors to my brother's flat which was closer to the East Gate.

A remarkable thing happened as I got indoors. Brother Bola listened to my story of how a full tin of milk was thrown at my eye almost making me blind. Surprisingly, I had not mentioned anything about suicide to him, but to my amazement he sat me down and started counseling me on the dangers of committing suicide.

It was as if he had a premonition of something bad that was to happen. He talked at length and told me to exercise some patience with Big Brother. He said I should have courage in the face of adversity; and concluded by saying I should not give up on life.

Hmm... *Yinkus mi*, I still have the scar of the eye that was almost blinded. Move nearer...

look at it! I am also being reminded of the day I nearly committed suicide. I cursed Big Brother that day in my agony and I evoked prophesy that one day, he would use his own hands to cause blindness for his children too.

It is said that whatever evil anyone does, their children would reap out of it indefinitely. Well, I think that curse later became a reality in the life of one of his children.

I heard from the grapevine of how Big Brother had slapped his son in anger and the boy became blind in one eye. I heard he was rushed to the hospital but the eye could not be saved. It became blind forever! I am so sure that the blindness would be a constant reminder to him too.

Chapter 8

I Wanted To Be Free

Days rolled over days and months climbed over months, the unpleasant situation in Big Brother's house was deteriorating. I had no life; he stole my self-worth. The more I stayed with him, the more he destroyed my self esteem.

Big Brother was the type of person that didn't know the meaning of a little bit of privacy; he was always looking through my things, questioning my activities and consistently bringing me down in the presence of his friends and members of our family. He called me horrible names and made me feel wrong about everything.

I had friends in school; sympathetic friends; friends who were my audience; those who were ever ready to listen to my story. I didn't mind the fact that they had nothing to contribute to me by way of advice or anything but I was contented with the fact that they were there to listen to my woeful stories and to empathize with me.

There was a period Big Brother told me that henceforth; there would be no food for me in the house. The one-meal-a-day luxury I used to have had been cancelled. I wondered where he wanted me to be eating when I didn't have any money of my own; I was just a secondary school student and not a working class man. Well, my friends became the shoulders I leaned on as they didn't allow hunger to whip me.

They offered me lunch in their different homes. Instead of going home straight, they made me to stop over for whatever food their mothers had prepared for them. They made sure I ate to my satisfaction before going back to the dungeon I called a home.

I remember that when the situation of money matter was unbearable, I had to sell my textbooks at give-away prices to fend for myself. These were the *pass-down* books from my brothers. I sold them one after the other to my fellow students. Life became bearable a little bit; at least I could buy cooked rice and beans to eat on the way to school early in the morning.

My favorite meal at that time was *Muke.* This was a local meal of mashed beans; the delicacy of the folks living in Osun State Nigeria, most especially the Ijesa native people. I also had enough left-over cash to take taxi to school early in the mornings, instead of the incessant trekking. I didn't mind the evening stroll back home; I wasn't the only student doing that.

Oh...! I should have told you earlier that along the line, Big Brother got married to a lovely and very quiet lady of Abeokuta*;* a town in Ogun State of Nigeria. I used to wonder why such a very nice lady like Aunty Funmi should be married to a beast like Big Brother. They had two boys...Kola and Bode. Many a times, his wife would quarrel with him to stop being cruel to me but big Brother would shout on her;

"Is he your brother? Why don't you mind your business? Abayomi is my responsibility and I can deal with him anyhow as I wish. I make all decisions about him and I don't want your input, okay? So keep to your lane!"

Big Brother's two sons grew up practically in my hands because I took great care of them from infancy. I did not transfer any aggression against their Father to them and many people used to give me the credit for that; I just could not bring myself to do evil to those innocent kids. I saw them as the younger siblings I never had. I told them many bedtime stories, I taught them songs and we shared secrets. I loved them dearly even though I hated their Dad with passion.

Anytime I was hurled in a corner crying from the beating of Big Brother, those children would come near me in their innocent nature and pat me on the head or rock me on the shoulders to empathize with me...

"Uncle Abayor, sorry...! Don't cry again, okay?"

At other times, they simply sat on both sides of me looking sorrowful without saying anything. In their silence, I used to regain strength because I felt I was not alone. Their father hated to see this scene of brotherly bonding we had. He would yell at them to leave me alone and that I should not rub a worthless destiny on his children.

During the period I was preparing for the General Certificate Examination (GCE), I approached Big Brother that I needed money to purchase GCE form to enable me sit for the exam. He sent me away with his usual abuse of a nonentity low lifer.

I begged him for three days consecutively to spare money for the Form but he would not hear of it. He saw it as a waste of resources as I would never do well in life. So I stopped asking. All my friends in school sat for the exam and some of them got admission into the University with the result.

It was a relief to be through with secondary school and I immediately went in search of a job. I needed money to sustain myself. Fortunately for me, I got a job as a clerical officer at the Local Government Council. I was excited; now I had money of my own!

Big Brother was not happy that I was financially independent. He wanted to be in control of my salary as well as my life. So, when I was paid the first salary, he came to demand for it saying my first salary was meant for him because he was the representative of our parents.

I was speechless! How could an elder be this callous? While I was in the Secondary school, I hardly got money to spend, if not for the fact that I sold my '*pass-down books*'....how would I have survived?

I ignored his stretched hand and kept mute. He gave me a dirty slap for ignoring him and barked at me to hand over the money to him but I refused. He was so annoyed that he issued a one month ultimatum for me to leave his house for good. He said my presence in his house was suffocating him. I was excited; I was over the moon.

Actually, that was not the first time of threatening me to leave his house for good. He had been doing it ever since I started living with him. But this time I decided enough was enough. I was ready to leave as I had money of my own.

I started making arrangement for where I would put up. I got a friend to share a room with and I was looking forward to freedom of life! A week to the expiration of the ultimatum, one of my brothers paid us a weekend visit. I confided in Brother Solomon that I would be leaving Big Brother's house for good. He asked what happened and I briefed him,

Brother Solomon had gone behind my back to spill the beans that I was packing to a friend's house in town. That night, Big Brother tongue lashed me so much for venturing to leave his house and I reminded him that he was the one who gave me the one month ultimatum.

"You think you can leave my house just as you wish? Who will do all the house chores while you are gone? Answer me...! If I see your leg outside of this house, I would personally kill you and nothing would happen. Stupid fool...! Who do you think you are"? He roared.

I stood rooted on the spot. How did this wicked man find out I was going to share a room with a friend? I decided to find out from Brother Solomon.

"Let me get this straight, Brother Solomon", I said sounding very puzzled. "Did you at any time discuss my case with Big Brother? Did you tell him the secret I kept with you"? I asked him as I gritted my teeth, trying to suppress my anger.

"Well--well...." Brother Solomon said, drumming his fingers on the table. "I am very sorry, Abayor, please forgive me."

He went on to defend himself as he felt compelled to do something about my leaving the house for an unknown destination. I was so angry! Prior to this, I had looked forward to enjoying my freedom away from this House of Hell.

I brooded over Brother Solomon's words all night and throughout the following day. Leaving the house would have been an answered prayer for me. I needed to be free; I needed my sanity. O yes...! I wanted out! I was the unpaid servant (House boy) in Big

Brother's house. I did all the jobs of any servant. He had even declared it in public sometime ago that I was his house boy.

Let me tell you that story. It happened that I was ill of malaria and Big Brother took me to the Hospital and we had to register for a card. His family card was only for his immediate family and his servants; any other wards that were not officially recognized would have to be registered separately and the treatment would not be free.

Big Brother felt he was not ready to waste his money on me and so, he would rather categorize me as his servant. The clerk at the Hospital desk found it hard to believe I was his servant. He kept on looking at the two of us. He must have seen the striking resemblance on our faces. I was so embarrassed that day!

Chapter 9

Upper Cut

Yinkus mi... I hope you are moving along with me in this story-telling with your mind's eye. You may want to know if I succeeded in escaping from the Lion's den I called a home or not. Yes, I did leave the house eventually.

There is an adage which says...However long it takes a fellow who stammers to call *baba* (Father); with persistence his goal would ultimately be achieved! In other words, people who are being physically abused as I had been should have faith in their future, if they persevere.

I enrolled at a certain Evening Classes known as Extra Moral Classes and paid my fees from my meager salary. I also bought JAMB Entrance Examination form and paid for my School Certificate Exam. My feeding, clothing and transport fares were taken care of from my salary as well. I managed my finances well to cover my needs. I was independent of anybody absolutely!

Some days before the commencement of JAMB exam, I had studied as if my life depended on the outcome of the result. Truly, my life depended on it because it was my ticket to freedom. If I passed, I would move to the next height and say bye-bye to Big Brother's house.

So, I hardly slept and was always studying. I had read overnight on the eve of the exam without sleeping a wink and had gone straight to the examination hall. I saw it as a 'war' that must be won! After the exam I came home with the hope of having a deserved rest only to find the door of the house firmly locked.

"Where are the children? Who locked the door"?

I asked no one in particular. I was shocked to find the situation that way. The back door was never locked before now to enable any of us have access into the house. If Big Brother was going to travel and I would be left at home, he always mentioned it. But this time, no one was at home. Where could they have gone?

I sat at the doorstep and rested my head on my knees. All sorts of thoughts crossed my mind; what if they didn't return that night? Here was I, desperately in need of a good sleep as I did not have a good sleep for two days consecutively. Thanks to my desperation to pass the almighty JAMB exam!

I must have sat there for hours and when I raised my head it was already dark. A look at my wrist watch told me that it was 7.30pm. I was convinced that they would not return to the house that night and I was too tired to trek to any of my friend's house to put up for the night. I was dog-tired!

About half an hour later, the house boy of a neighbor came to inform me that his Madame would like to see me. I followed him to Mama Bukola's house. It was there that I saw my two nephews in their pajamas playing with the Agbede's children. I was pleasantly surprised. The Madam's name was Mrs. Agbede and she asked me what I did wrong to have made Big Brother to warn her not to hand over the key of the house to me.

This meant that Big Brother deliberately wanted me to sleep outside. The woman saw how tired I was and my eyeballs were red and bloodshot. She took pity on me and gave me the key to the house.

I slept like a log of wood all through the night until I was rudely woken up by a heavy banging on the door, the following morning. It was Big Brother...! He had arrived and gone to collect the key only to be told I was indoors.

He was vehemently abusing and cursing me for having the opportunity to sleep indoors when his plan was for me to suffer and sleep outside. He nearly pulled down the roof of the house saying I should bring out the girl I had with me in the house. I just stood there watching his moves; my eyes were still dim of sleep.

He was not alone. He came with a friend. His friend stood beside him and said;

"No, Diekola, look at the boy's face. This boy has been sleeping deeply. Look at him now..."?

"What stupid sleep could that have been? The way we banged this door should have woken a dead person in the mortuary, yet he didn't come out on time"!

That was Big Brother for you; always putting me down in the presence of his friends. He pushed me irritably out of the way and I fell down. He was looking around for the 'imaginary' girl that was supposed to be in the house with me.

I was not expecting a push and I was too weak of fatigue. So the push was an antidote that cleared the sleep from my eyes at that instant. I couldn't make a head or tail about what he was saying. I returned to my room to continue my sleep because I had a splitting headache.

Some hours later, Big Brother came to the room and shouted at me again to get up and tidy the house. I did, but I was sick and dizzy, compounded by the throbbing headache I had. I told him I was ill and any chores would have to wait until I was better. Out of the blues, I saw his arms rise over his head. His slatted eyes glared at me. His teeth were gritted through his dark beard.

Then he struck, swiftly, before I had a chance to stabilize. He was beating my shoulders and head with the leg of a broken chair. I wasn't quick enough but I fell down. He kept on beating and kicking me at the same time. He called me a lot of horrible names.

With the beatings he gave me; I saw stars splashing out of my eyes in many different colors. I let out a shrieking call for help! His wife rushed in but Big Brother signaled to her to leave the room.

As I kept on screaming and weeping, he was shouting that out of his entire brothers, I was the only one that had wronged him so badly. That phrase used to puzzle me till this day. What did I do wrong?

Anytime he was in deep anger, he would say I was the only one who had offended him among his brothers. I was tired of hearing it. He went on and on telling me I was worth nothing in this world and saying all sorts of derogatory words to me.

I lay on the floor and was so well beaten and fagged out. Blood flowed across my face and I could taste it in my mouth. I heard his voice faintly screaming back at me;

"I will kill you, Abayomi! I will make sure I kill you with my hands!"

Like a bolt of a lightning, I stood up and pulled at his shirt and it got torn. I didn't know what gave me the boldness that day to stand up to him; maybe because I was tired and fed up of his wickedness. He was shocked to see my reaction and it showed on his face.

He removed his belt and gave me several lashes in a row. I was using my hands to protect my head and my eyes; I had to do this because he loved to target my head anytime he was wild like this. I still have not forgotten that he nearly made me blind--once bitten twice shy.

I got the beating of my life! Big Brother used me as a punching bag that night. Each punch was like a sledge hammer being banged on my shoulders and chest. When he was done with boxing, he kicked me and I fell down. I was rolling on the floor while he was kicking me angrily.

My face, my cheeks and lips were swollen. I was puffed up as if a trailer vehicle ran over me. My arms and laps were not spared either; they were blood-shot and had become red and black in colors. I cried so much to the extent that I was worn out and helpless.

Big Brother too was exhausted and was breathing as if he ran a marathon race. It was then he left me alone. He looked at his torn shirt and got more irritated. He bent down and pulled me up by the neck. He put his face to my face and gnashed is teeth at me;

"You have the effrontery to lay your hands on me and tear my shirt? You...? Hah... I can bet it with you, this is your last night in this house. If you stay a minute longer I will kill you and nothing will happen". He threatened!

Big Brother was a deadly enemy and he meant every threat. I rose up quickly in spite of all the pains in my body and my swollen lips. I rushed to the room and threw a few shirts and trousers in my traveling bag; I didn't forget to pack some of my books. I checked at the time, it was 11.40pm.

I ran out of the house as if my feet were on fire. Everywhere was dark and chilling. I was walking briskly, looking left and right and reciting Psalm23--"The Lord is my Shepherd, I shall not want..."

I had gone some distance when I met the Night Watchmen. I was frightened to the roots of my hair. I froze in my tracks and my heart was beating so loudly that I could hear it. As a fact, it is not a child's play to meet those sternly looking men at the thick of the night. It is their modus operandi to be unsympathetic to night crawlers.

They could terrorize anyone found walking in the night and the types of punishment meted on culprits are always very demeaning and humiliating. The men were those that should be called "Raiders of the night!"

On this night, I was frightened because I thought they would subject me to that degrading punishment of carrying a big stone on my head and be doing midnight market advertising while chanting;

"I am selling delicious bean cakes; buy one take one free".

The culprit would be made to shout on top of his voice. If the voice was not loud enough, he would be thoroughly beaten. He would follow them around the neighborhood till dawn when he would be released to go his way. I prayed they wouldn't subject me to that degrading act.

I greeted those men with utmost respect and I tearfully explained to them that I was sent out of the house. I didn't forget to whip up emotions by telling them that my parents died the same day and I was asked to stay with someone who wanted me dead. This person gave me ultimatum to leave his house or be dead before morning.

I told them how I was beaten mercilessly. One of the four night guards beamed his touch to my face and saw the tell-tale signs of brutality--my swollen jaw, the blood-shot and teary eyes, my swollen upper lips and running nose.

They all pitied me and wondered why I should be sent out of the house at that ungodly hour. One of them suggested that I should go back home. If I was allowed to go wherever I was going, I might meet another set of vicious Night watchmen who would not be so kind-hearted to set me free. They agreed to walk me back home. They reckoned that it would be safer for me to sit at our doorstep till dawn.

I sat at a corner near the house, waiting for the break of the day. At the crack of dawn, I went to Ayodele's house to brief her of the incidence. Ayodele was my girlfriend who had supported me with her kind words in the past few years of our relationship.

I later went to my friend's house (Bukoye) to have my bath and get set for the office. Bukoye was not surprised to see me. He had been expecting that I would be thrown out of the house sooner than later with my brother's constant threat of quit notice.

At work, I took permission and went to see the Doctor. This was a different Consultant aside of the Family Doctor of Big Brother's. The Doctor was astonished at my battered face. He lifted up my face gently and looked at the bruises. With a deep frown on his face, he asked me gently;

"Who on earth did this to you? Who beat you up like this"?

I kept mute and was looking at the floor. How was I to tell him I was beaten as if I was an armed robber that was caught red-handed? He asked again and I told a lie that I slipped and knocked my face on the wall.

He must have known it was a lie because he stood up and asked me to get on the examination table and remove my shirt. I did and he saw laceration of lashes all over my body. There were fresh swollen wounds on my chest, shoulders and neck as well. He asked me again;

"Did you say you slipped on the floor or were you beaten"?

"I slipped, Sir. It was a big fall". I maintained a straight face and answered in a very sober voice.

Doctor Beckley shook his head and went back to his table. He prescribed some drugs and I left.

By the time I returned from the Hospital, Brother Bola was there waiting for me in my office. Words had gotten to him that I had left Big Brother's house. I made the move to open my mouth to tell him all that happened but as usual he asked me not to say anything. I tried to show him my wounds but he didn't want to see them. I guessed he was near tears himself and was trying not to break down in my presence.

He offered me a better accommodation somewhere in town. He got in contact with an Agent and paid the rent fee of a year. I was given the keys and we went out together to locate the place.

I was excited and I moved in immediately. It was so peaceful to live without constant shouts of abuses, humiliation and curses. I had time to study very well for my School

Certificate Examination as a private student. I read so hard mainly to prove to Big Brother that I was not a dullard and that I could make my papers if I had time to study well without distraction.

I did brilliantly well in my exam and got distinction in all the papers I sat for. My JAMB Examination result was released thereafter; it was a feather to my cap. I resigned from work and prepared for the admission into the University of Ife as it was known then, to study Metallurgical Engineering.

Chapter 10

I Joined the League

I became a student in the prestigious University of Ife as we called it then. My eldest Sister, Tundun had promised to give me scholarship that would cover all my expenses at the University. I was excited and I grabbed the opportunity with both hands. There was a ray of light that was going to make life bearable for me. Unfortunately, the ray of light was deemed when after the first year of that scholarship, Sister Tundun had to withdraw it from me.

She came to me at the end of that session to say that her husband would be going back to school to read for his Bachelors in Sociology and her family would likely be cash-strapped if my scholarship was not withdrawn. In other words, she left me high and dry! I was dumbfounded! Where was I to get the fund to see me through school?

I went to one of my brothers, Wale and asked for his financial assistance. He too was not buoyant but he paid my tuition for that year and I went back to school.

I decided to strap my belt tight and find a way to fund my education. For starters, I relocated to the Staff Quarters through the help of a friend who introduced me to a very nice couple.

I asked them for an accommodation and the Professor just took a liking to me and offered me the use of his Boys' Quarters. It was not pre-arranged; I was assisting the family to do their laundry. They in turn were feeding me and giving me a weekly pocket money. I also got Bursary from the State Government that same year. Life became bearable!

I joined the league of Quarters boys; I had friends and I pretended to belong to a high fliers' club. I decided to make more money for myself by doing all types of odd jobs here and there. It was at that instance that I decided to turn my hobby-- Public Speaking, to money making venture. I was in search of anything to do to pay my fees and fund my upkeep. I wanted money at all cost!

One day, some guys came to me and dropped a lot of money in an envelope on my laps. They said it was for me. I was curious; what was the money for? They would not say. They said only the Initiates were allowed to know the source of the money and since I was not a member, there was no need to tell me.

They said if I was a member of their Guild I would be given a hundred fold of that amount. My eyes and ears popped out at the mention of money. What fraternity could that be? Without thinking, I signified my intention to join as long as I would be given easy money to augment my expenses.

From that day on, I waved good-bye to poverty from my life on Campus and I was no more doing any menial jobs. I became a big boy and lived a flamboyant life. I bought a Haley Davidson power bike and cruised around with it, mostly to oppress and woo the female folks. I used it for a session and bought another one--a Kawasaki Z1000 bike.

Thereafter, I had the boldness to talk to girls; there was money to spend and my club to service. Our meeting place was somewhere in town with our sponsors and we paid our dues!

Yinkus mi... you were on the campus with me at that time, so, you already know my story from that end. I don't need to recap it. You were one of my very close friends back then. We journeyed through the campus together on my bike but I still can't fathom why you refused to fall in love with me despite my easy flow of money.

I could only guess it was the unalloyed attention that your boyfriend was giving you at the time. What's his name again...? Hmm...? I remember people called him by his initials... Did you get married to him eventually? Anyway, let us not digress. This is my story I am recapping and I still have the floor!

My girlfriend, Mary-Anne and I were an item; we had a nice time spending the money with reckless abandon while we were in school. After the expiration of our studies we left the

Campus for our mandatory National Youth Service Corp of one year program; mine was at Port -Harcourt while Mary-Anne was posted to Kano. We were writing letters frequently to each other pledging our undying love and suddenly the brook got dried up; Mary Anne stopped writing.

I had to take a plane to Kano to locate her through the address she gave me during our correspondence. The Youth Corps members that were there informed me that she had relocated to another address; she no longer lived with them.

It was a Great IFE alumnus and also a member of the Palm-wine Drinkers' Club I saw in Kano town that let me into the picture. He said that Mary-Anne had found herself a rich Hausa merchant who had made her his fourth wife; after all, I had not yet given her a ring, so I could not lay any claim on her.

I got the address and located her. She was all covered up with a veil. As soon as she came to the gate to check who it was that asked of her, she screamed on sighting me.

It was as if she saw a ghost and fled indoors as fast as her legs could carry her. I knew at that instant that I had lost Mary-Anne for good. I got back to Port-Harcourt to pick up the pieces of my life.

I later received a letter from Mary-Anne urging me to look for my missing rib elsewhere as she had found hers in the Alhaji in whose house I came the other time. I was extremely down in the dumps for many weeks. It seemed as if the world was crashing down on me. Here was a girl I had built my hopes on; it was during this time of depression that I found the Lord with the help of a Christian sister.

This lovely Christian Sister in the Lord came every Sunday to minister about Jesus to me early in the mornings and to invite me to their Church. At first, I was being civil and would endure her preaching. I did that for a couple of weeks until I gave her a nod and followed her to her church. It was there I gave my life to Christ and I was encouraged to go for Rudiments in Bible Teachings, which I did. I also went for Baptism and Deliverance ministrations.

Sister Linda, for that was her name, was always with me. She came around often to preach and follow me up in the Lord. One day, the scales on my eyes fell off and I perceived her attractiveness. Slowly but surely, we entered into a relationship.

By the time the Youth Corp Service year was over, we were already in love and planning our future together. Many of my Youth Corp colleagues decided to return to their States at the expiration of our Service Year, but as for me, I had no home to return to. I made Port-Harcourt my home base, more so when my wife to-be was an indigene.

One significant thing happened to me that needed to be told. I found out that after I left the Campus, I had become impotent but I put it down on examination fatigue. There was no way to find out if I was healed or not since I had become born again and I was not expected to sleep around. All through our courtship, Linda and I did not go into sexual activities because my new found faith was against it. My favorite song at that time was this;

The unclean things I used to do, I do them no more

The rough places I used to go, I go there no more

The strong drinks I used to drink, I drink them no more

There is a great change since I became born again

The bad friends I used to keep, I keep them no more

The foul things I used to say, I say them no more

The weeds I used to smoke, I smoke them no more

There is a great change since I became born again"

Chapter 11

The Wind Has Blown

We got married in Port-Harcourt. It was a quiet matrimony. I got a lucrative job in one of the oil companies in Port-Harcourt and life was favorable to us. I loved my wife affectionately to a fault; I spoilt her with everything money could buy and she was the envy of her friends. I must say that she too was a dedicated wife who took her vows to the letter.

I had thought after our wedding the impotency would be a thing of the past but I was mistaken. It was as if an evil eye was casted on me. Much as I tried to fulfill my conjugal duties on our matrimonial bed, I was like a boiled vegetable at the nick of time of action and at every other time. This gave the two of us a very serious concern and the several medical practitioners we consulted did all they could but no respite. They always told us that there was nothing wrong with me. I prayed and fasted but there was no improvement in our situation.

Linda took it all in her strides and was prayerful and hopeful. She did not for once regret marrying me. She, it was who took it upon herself to go round all Prayer Mountain Churches in supplication to our plight. Her family was worried that we were not able to start our own family. They constantly stressed Linda to tell them what was happening, but Linda would only say we were looking unto God for the right time; as the saying goes, God's time is the best.

I could say I was the culprit as far as her inability to get pregnant was concerned but I never told Linda about it. After a marathon prayer session one day, I had a dream where I saw myself in the midst of my old friends whom we were in the same club together. I saw us "jumping the fire".

Actually, jumping the fire was one of our ritual activities in the cult. We always felt a burning sensation in our groins for a few hours after the jump. *Yinkus,* I don't feel inclined to talk much on this. I hope you will understand. Please don't make me explain the meaning of it. Okay?

Could this be the reason for my impotency? Was I the only one involved or could it be a collective occurrence? There was no way to find out; it had been years since I left the Campus. I kept this revelation to myself and Linda had no inkling about it.

My hands were like the Midas touch in Port-Harcourt. Whatever I touched turned to gold; I mean I was really blessed financially. I worked like a jackal and money was flowing. My wife was pampered but the joy of marriage was missing and this casted a shadow to our bliss.

I am a very caring husband that any woman would love to have. There are no house chores I could not do despite the fact that I am wealthy. Remember my life experiences with Big Brother...

Years rolled into years and we had clocked ten years in marriage. I was still like a boiled vegetable but Linda's faith remained strong believing that I would be healed in God's time. There were continuous interferences from her family and we planned to relocate. I felt a new environment could do us good. We put machinery into place and eventually left Port-Harcourt for Ibadan.

We settled down fast and my business picked up considerably and money started flowing again. I built this house that we are in, within the second year that we relocated to Ibadan and Linda called it a Palace because of its magnificence. I was still impotent. I was worried but hopeful that God would forgive me for joining the cult while in school.

Somehow, as years sped by, I got in touch with one of my old paddies whom we *"jumped the fire"* together. I wanted to find out if they were in the same boat as I was. I learnt out of the ten of us, only four were unable to procreate. I was convinced in my heart of hearts that it was the consequences of jumping the fire in our time of ignorance that affected our inability to be virile.

One of us is Tosin who is in Diaspora. We communicated through Facebook inbox one day and we chatted at length on the calamity that had befallen us due to our ignorance of joining a cult that trapped us into this death sentence of impotency. I did not delete our conversation before sleeping off. I only put the laptop to sleep mode. Later in the night, Linda needed to use my laptop as hers was malfunctioning. She switched it on and the conversation page came into view. She had no choice than to read it.

Linda was not a woman to scout through my Facebook, phone, Laptop or diary in search of exhibit to nail me. She always took permission before poking into my privacy and I respected her privacy too. It was a mutual thing between us.

All I knew was that I woke up the following day and found Linda on the bed with my laptop on. She was staring at it. I rose up quickly to check the page she was staring at. I found the chat that Tosin and I wrote, telling me about the cause of our impotence. Could you believe that?

Sleep cleared from my eyes immediately. I grabbed my laptop from Linda and switched it off. I stood up and moved closer to my wife but she would have none of me.

I begged and cried for forgiveness but her mind was made up to break up with me after 28years of marriage. The two of us were weeping bitterly as if we were mourning a dead relation.

She said I betrayed the trust she had in me for years. She had been with me through thick and thin and she carried the cross of barrenness stoically to the detriment of her family and friends. She was faithful to her marital vows before God and man, despite her inability to conjugal rights for many years. I didn't deem it fit to confide in her.

Linda was ready to separate with me immediately. I pleaded with her to give me a second chance. She declined any form of entreaty. I offered money. She rejected to collect a dime from me saying it was blood money. I appealed to her that my money was a clean one; I had worked very hard to be where I found myself today and I had no skeleton in my wardrobe.

I had worked diligently to build an empire of my business. What we had on the Campus was just a youthful exuberance of belonging to a naughty cult. We never knew the repercussion would be so devastating like this. We were just fooling around!

Without wasting any more time, Linda brought out suitcases and started throwing her clothes in them. She refused to listen to all I was saying. Her mind was made up to break up from me. All the while, she was wailing and speaking in her native dialect. Helplessly, I stood aside to watch my wife of 28years as she packed her belongings in suitcases and I could do nothing to stop her.

Oh, I should have mentioned it earlier that we had a housemaid--a very young girl who was about sixteen years old when she first came to live with us. Her mother died when she was in the secondary school and her father remarried. After her School Certificate Examination, she opted to look for a job so that she could be away from her home.

It was Linda who insisted that she wanted a maid in the house. I didn't want any intruder in our home and I objected to having a maid. Anyway, the maid started living with us and I didn't hide my dislike for her. I made a rule for her not to touch my food or anything that had to do with me. I terrorized her, so to speak; just like the way Big Brother did to me in those days.

The exchanged of words that Linda and I had, made the poor girl to eavesdrop on us. She rushed to Linda, knelt before her and grabbed her legs crying profusely. She was pleading with her not to leave. Meanwhile I was on my knees too at the other edge of the bed imploring her to consider the love I had for her.

I could not control the tears that were dropping from my eyes. I was crying like a baby as I watched my life tumbling down. Linda too fell into a passion of weeping; it was really a competition of tears!

I loved Linda and I could not think of any other woman besides her. We complimented each other and I had grown deeply attached to her. For 28years she bore the burden of not sexually active with me, her husband;

and now-- the reality of the fact that I was the offender. It was a blow to her. She was really a good wife and a faithful companion. This unforeseen calamity had upset her terribly.

Linda had pulled a chair close to the small writing table in our bedroom and slumped face-down against the wood. One arm cradled her head while the other was stretched in front of her as her body shook with utterly abandoned weeping. I had never seen her like this and I was appalled. I tried to say something comforting, but nothing stemmed the flow of her racking sobs.

The three of us in the room were sobbing; each of us with different reasons. The maid kept saying she didn't wish to be sent back to her father whom she had not seen for all the years she had been working for us. She had been with us for five years at that time and had seen Linda as her family because my wife loved her like a relation. So her weeping was understandable.

Later, Linda got up after she was spent. Her weeping subsided and she went about packing her things without minding us. Apparently, she didn't sleep throughout the night as soon as she read the Facebook inbox messages. She had a deep thinking on the steps to take that midnight and came to a conclusion to break up with me. Her large suitcases were five in number. She didn't pack all her things but the most important.

She sat in the living room with her suitcases at her feet. She had stopped crying and was staring into space. Feeling helpless and inadequate, I knelt beside her and held her hands without saying anything. Maybe I could have said something if I hadn't felt just as bad myself.

We were like this for many minutes; it was peaceful and comforting in a way. I was looking intently at her as if I was memorizing every feature on her face. As the saying goes, if you love someone, that means you have to let them go, if that is what they want. A telephone call came through for her that a truck was at our gate. The house maid was sent to open the gate.

It dawn on the poor girl that Linda was leaving for good, so she made a last minute spirited persuasion to make my wife have a change of mind. It was in futile; no amount of pleading could stop Linda my wife, my jewel, my soul mate of 28years...The ship had sailed and the bridge burnt down!

Linda held the maid's hands and told her to look after herself. She then moved to where I stood and came into my arms and I held her, whispering words which meant nothing. Her slim body was pressed against me and I kissed her lips and face and hair and I felt hot tears on her cheeks.

For some minutes, none of us talked, only the rise and fall of her sobbing could be heard. Gradually, her weeping ended. Her body relaxed against mine and she made no move to break away. As I held her in my arms, my mind kept on insisting: "Don't let her go"! Yet I could hear another voice in me saying: "Release her"!

So I pushed her gently away to look at her face again. I put my hand under her chin and lifted her face towards mine. There were tears in the corners of her eyes. A look of pain came and went in her eyes.

"Linda dear, where are going? I will think of a way to make everything all right. Breaking away from me is not the solution. Please my darling..."

I knew that whatever I said would make no difference. The hopelessness must have been apparent in my voice. She began to cry again, hiding her face from me. I heard her words faintly: "It is over Abayor...Over"!

Her matter-of-fact tone didn't surprise me. In twenty-eight years of our marriage, I had learnt that she had a way of dismissing unpleasant situations from her mind. At times I found it maddening, because things that bothered her never get resolved.

She gave my cheek an absent kiss and stepped out of the house. She entered her car and drove off with the truck full of her belongings driving behind her. I couldn't bear to watch her leave so I didn't see her off. When she had gone, I stood quite still at the center of the living room listening. I was hoping she would turn the car round and come back home. I was hopelessly hopeless!

I felt the muscles in my throat tightening; bursting spreading knots of pain which brought moisture to my eyes. I looked about me; it was as if I was dreaming. I was not prepared for this occurrence. The floodgate of tears was opened again and was rolling down my cheeks freely. I didn't bother to wipe it.

Our housemaid came indoors and knelt down at a corner as if she was serving punishment. She was looking at me with fright written all over her face. I must have stood at the same spot for hours, with reminiscences of Linda and of our years together in my mind. I had loved my wife with all my soul and my being. I shook myself to reality; the girl was still on her knees crying softly and looking at me.

This maid must have been very terrified of what my pronouncement of her fate would be. She was aware I didn't fancy the idea of her living in the house; I didn't hide the fact, even to her face.

If I could have my way, I would have sent the girl packing long ago. This had made the poor girl to be very jittery of me; she would scamper to a corner any time I was in the same place with her in the house. I didn't hide the disdain for her at all. Looking at her irritated me so much. Now, Linda left her with me in the house. The girl was expecting me to bark at her like I always did and send her away to wherever she came from. But I was so emotionally drained to even bark at anybody! I was extremely sad and my mind was in turmoil.

The lyrics of the song by Whitney Houston drifted across my mind as I stood looking into space.

I will Always Love You

And I ...will always love you uu...

Will always love you!

Chapter 12

Paradigm Shift

My experiences with Big Brother years back, reflected on the way I behaved towards our housemaid. I just couldn't stand her presence in the house. Unfortunately, I found myself behaving just like the bully of my Big Brother but not too much of a cruel way.

I turned to look at the maid for a second, thinking of how best to dismiss her, but I was too weak to even lift a finger. The emotions had sapped all my energy; I just hissed at her and went upstairs to continue brooding over my calamity.

Prior before the incident, it was my habit to mount the stairs two or three steps at a time, but on this day, I trailed upwards like an old man slightly breathless, throat tight, and eyes prickling. I cursed myself for being a sentimental fool by not deleting all my correspondences that landed me in this deep shit of trouble. I didn't come down throughout that day and I did not eat either. The following day I was still in bed and didn't come down. I had switched off all my phones and was incommunicado with everyone; I didn't go to work nor contacted the management, after all, as the Chief Executive Officer I could pull stunts. I didn't have the drive to move on with life anymore.

My Staff didn't see me for two days and couldn't get me on the phone. A powerful delegation was sent to the house by the third day. It was early in the morning and I heard cars zooming into the compound. I looked out of the window and saw my deputy and other managerial team on the terrace. They came to find out about me.

The Housemaid in her wisdom covered my inadequacies. I heard from where I stood at the window sill as she told them that my wife had travelled and I had been ill for quite a while. The people asked if they could see me but she said she had the strict instruction from my family Doctor not to allow anyone disturb my sleep.

She assured them that I was getting better gradually and that I needed the rest. She also added that it was the Doctor that switched off my phones. They nodded knowingly and told her to pass their best wishes of speedy recovery to me. I watched all of them leave one after the other from my bedroom window.

I was impressed by what this girl did. Another girl in her shoes would have spilt the beans. Meanwhile, I was praying fervently and seeking the face of God on my knees. To say the truth, I didn't deserve a lifetime of unhappiness for one mistake I made. I had not tasted anything for the last three days. I felt light-headed.

Anyway, I came downstairs to request for tea without milk. She made the tea and added a few slices of toasted bread beside it. I only took the tea and thanked her. On my way upstairs, she stopped me halfway of the stairs;

"Sir, can I cook a little rice for you?"

She asked in a very timid and quiet voice. When Linda was around this girl had never touched my food. I turned round and shouted a loud No! I left her gawping and I went upstairs.

I was praying all day asking God for healing so as to have Linda back into my life. I prayed like never before and was even doing personal deliverance--binding and casting out demons of impotency and asking for God's forgiveness. I had challenged God to do the miraculous about my case; my manhood must be restored to me!

All through the nine days of fasting and praying, I was only taking tea and water! By the 10th day in the afternoon, I was weak and frail.

I felt exhausted to the point of sickness. The light-headed feeling was persistent now; I felt fatigued and weak, but not hungry.

In the mirror before me, I saw a face recognizable as my own and yet strangely different. I looked like a man in an emotional shock; I saw a caricature of myself. There were tiny lines in the corners of my eyes and

I needed to shave badly as the hair on my chin and jaw had grown so much. I found a shaving stick and I began to soap my face.

I came downstairs and made pap for myself and sat in the living room. I was there for the whole day, just staring into space and sipping the pap. I was reviewing every step of my summation. Linda...! Linda left me high and dry. Where do I go from here? A thick, hard lump burned in my throat, making it impossible to swallow. I was within inches of tears again.

I got tired and slept off till nightfall. The Housemaid came indoors and put on the light. As soon as she saw me, she screamed loudly of fright. She thought she saw an apparition. I woke up rudely and asked what was going on. She knelt down and said she thought I was a ghost. She moved nearer and asked the inevitable question; if I wanted her to still be a maid in the house.

She had to ask as she wanted to know if she was still relevant. I looked at her for a long while. In as much as I hated the services of house helps, I didn't want this girl to go away. I was impressed by the way she handled the officials from the office. I sat up and told her to carry on with her job if she wanted to stay. She was excited and was praying all kinds of prayers for me.

I was beside myself with amusement and when she eventually stopped, I asked her to prepare dinner for me; a very soft *amala* and *ewedu* soup. She was visibly shocked as I had never allowed her to touch my food. I ate heartily and that made the young girl happy. My energy to face the world came after the 10th day and I went back to work.

Gradually, I picked up the pieces of my life and I was my old self again. I promised myself not to go after any girl until I was healed of my impotency. My outing was restricted; I spent much of the time in front of the TV and with my Computer.

Several months had passed after Linda had left and I had adjusted to a life without a wife. I saw the maid only twice a day; once when she served the breakfast...if I wasn't fasting and at dinner. I had become very religious more than in the past years.

On a certain day, I didn't see her in the morning and I left for work. Normally, I would have heard the maid moving about in the kitchen, but this day I heard nothing. And when I arrived home in the evening, she was not at her kitchen post like she always did.

The following day, she had put breakfast on the table but she was nowhere to be found; same thing happened in the evening...the food was on the table but she was not around. I thought she was doing "Hide and Seek game", so I left it at that. You never know with women!

By the end of the third day, I decided to check her at the Boys' Quarters. What I saw terrified me in no small way. The door was locked from the inside and after several knocks on the door all I heard was some murmurings that were inaudible. I tried to peep but it was impossible and I turned to go back to the main building.

As I took a step, the murmuring sounded again. That was when I called out to her to open the door but she didn't. She was trying to say something that my ears couldn't pick. Several evil thoughts went through my mind; she couldn't be dead, I could hear her faint sound and her laborious breathing. It just occurred to me; she might be in danger. Three powerful kicks in quick succession brought the door down.

This girl was wrapped up in many clothes and was as hot as boiling water. The room was stinking of vomit which was spooled beside her bed. Her eyes were pale and sickly. For a few seconds, I stood transfixed to the spot, wondering what to do. I got my bearing right quickly and picked her up in my arms and carried her to the main house.

I left her on the couch in the living room and went round to get towel and a bowl of water. She was weeping silently and I put my arms around her for a few minutes. She pissed brown urine, a sign that she had malaria. I cleaned her up and placed a cold compress on her forehead to reduce the high temperature.

"Motunrayo, what happened to you? Talk to me!" My voice sounded as if it belonged to someone else. I was so afraid.

Poor girl! She was unable to talk but wouldn't stop crying. I felt a rush of sympathy for her. I forced her to take some plain tea. It didn't stay in her stomach as she vomited a yellowish mash. The spool reminded me of a child's diarrhea. There was a rotten smell in the air but there was no time to clean it up. I had to take her to the Hospital as fast as I could. All through the journey, I kept on praying for her to be alive. I knew that if I lost her I could be in trouble and would be a most unhappy man.

A remarkable thing happened at the Hospital. This girl had never had any illness to the point of being admitted in the Hospital since she started living with us. The minor illnesses she had were treated by the Pharmacy drug store in the neighborhood. Well, Linda never told me of any history of illness concerning the girl.

The Record Clerk at the Card section of the Hospital asked of my relationship with the girl while filling the Patient's case file. My mind flashed to when I was younger and Big Brother had brought me to their College Hospital where he told the Clerk that I was his house help. I knew how degrading it was when he referred to me as his House help. I would not make the same mistake with this girl now.

"She is my niece, my brother's daughter and she lives with me." I blurted out.

"What's her name Sir?" The Clerk asked.

I was thrown off balance. I only knew her first name. Since Linda brought her to live with us, I didn't bother to find out about her surname or where she came from. I had no idea who her parents were. I got my wits together quickly and gave the maid my surname; I had announced her to be my niece, so she could as well acquire my surname; Motunrayo Durogbajo!

She was admitted in the hospital and I moved towards the Exit. Several other people got on the elevator with me. We stood there waiting for the elevator to discharge us at the Ground Floor. A man standing close to me was covering his nose. As a matter of fact, I hate the antiseptic hospital smell too. I really don't fancy being in the hospital. The moment you become a patient, you lose your identity and you become a "case".

I came back home. I went straight to the Boys' Quarters to get fresh changing clothes for her to take back with me to the Hospital. I also tidied up the vomit mess and mopped and disinfected the whole room and the main house too. I couldn't believe myself that I was actually cleaning my house maid's room!

Motunrayo was diagnosed to have typhoid fever in its severe stage and was put under intensive care. I prayed like never before for her recovery. I could not lose that feeling of panic. How would I explain to anybody if she gave up the ghost?

I made several trips daily, shuttling between my office and the hospital; I only came home to take changing clothes and prepare food. It was after two weeks of being in the Hospital before Motunrayo could get her bearing and was able to recognize me.

She was there for a total of eight weeks before she was discharged. She had lost so much weight and was looking frail and tired. I paid all the bills and brought her home. In the car on our way home she just blurted out;

"My name is Motunrayo Ajadi *ooo*...and I am a native of Saki in Oyo State". The next words were long in coming. "I know who I am."

I shifted my gaze off the road to look at her as I was driving and I smiled. I got her point. She must have heard the Doctors and Nurses referring to her as Motunrayo Durogbajo. She might want an explanation from me for christening her a name against her wish.

"Brilliant girl ...!" I slammed my palms on the steering pretending to clap for her! "I guess you are now well enough to demand for an explanation in a subtle way. Hmm...? Where were you when the Record's clerk wanted to fill your name on the Hospital card? Your spirit had gone to your home town then. What did you call it? Saki... Am I right?" I asked jokingly.

"Yes Sir." She nodded brightly. "I'm from *Isale Ogun* in Saki town. My Mum is from *Ago-Are*, not too far from Saki. I was...." She started coughing.

"*Pele....* Take it easy. You may drink some water in the bottle. Don't say anything again. I will get to know more about your parents when you have fully recovered. Meanwhile, rest your back very well on the seat."

The two of us were lost in our thoughts. In the silence that followed, her laborious breathing was too loud. I couldn't but give God the praise for allowing the cup to pass over me! I looked at her yet again; she had shut her eyes and looked peaceful. Thank God she survived this illness. If not for the mercy of God, what would I have been saying now?

"Motunrayo, you must forgive my forwardness. If I regard you as a daughter and I speak to you as a father; that is because I am old enough to fill that role".

She gave me her sweetest smile and then looked away. I stole a glance at her from the corner of my eye and I found her smiling into space and shaking her head. This girl had seemed to be a pleasant child, amusing with her dialect of a typical local girl.

"You are smiling, Motunrayo. Let me just say a penny for your thoughts." I said. "What are you thinking of?"

"Hmmm... *Oga*! Are you interested in what I am thinking about?"

"Sure."

"You see, Sir, when your face is relaxed, your eyes are very sad."

"No. I don't mean them to be. I don't think of myself as being sad."

"Alright then... Sir".

"Motunrayo, do you know that I'd wanted to ask you about the story of your life since my wife dumped you with me? But it took the illness of typhoid that could have killed you to make it happen."

"You never asked me, Sir," she said evasively. "*Oga*, maybe you are not aware of it, but there is a definite signal you release on your face. It is like a placard that says, "Do Not Disturb". ... Therefore, I just keep to my lane."Motunrayo said.

"I can understand that. But that is not what we are talking about. I was very embarrassed at the hospital when I was being called to give your vitals...your name, age, town, allergic reactions and so on. I didn't know anything about you. I didn't know any of your relations. I was just praying that you would not die on me."

Motunrayo laughed out loud and said she would tell me all about herself when we get home. She became very quiet again with a deep frown on her face. The frown made deep crease lines in her forehead and around her eyes.

My mind went back again to Linda as it had always done since she left me. I had tried several times to erase her memory in my head but it was hard for me to do. If she was around, it would have been her responsibility to clear the mess of this housemaid. An idea started to form in my head but I pushed it back. How I missed my wife! A sense of blank despair swept over me. I felt desolate. I missed the company of Linda so much. I shook myself to reality and I turned to look sideways. I realized that my faith was being put to test. I couldn't but sing this song;

God of the Mountain--- by Linda Randle

"...For the God of the mountain, is still God in the valley

When things go wrong, He'll make them right..."

Chapter 13

A Constant Reminder

I did not allow the Housemaid to return to her room at the Boys' Quarters yet. I wanted her to be in the main house so that I could keep an eye on her until she was strong enough to go back there. She had a major surgery and the Doctor had warned that she was not to do any strenuous work or lift any load. She was to be under intensive care with a good supervision. So she moved to the visitor's room downstairs and I made her comfortable.

It was so amusing that I found myself in a paradigm shift of pampering and nursing my own housemaid, making her food and cleaning the house and even bath-toweling her for the first few days she got back home from the hospital.

Motunrayo's convalescence was a long one. She was subject to headaches and fits of dizziness; she had grown pale and thin. I began to look after this girl daily; she was my responsibility in spite of everything. She was purring with satisfaction anytime I entered her new room to either give her food or administer her medication.

I had to get myself psyched up to believe that she was my niece truly now and not a house maid any longer. It was then I could do what I had to do for her without feeling bad. In spite of her ill health, she was still determined to go back to her house chores.

Days rolled into weeks and I found myself enjoying the time spent with her. I would not remember how it happened but I got endeared to this girl. It was as if I had known her for a very long time.

She regained her strength and was able to move around the house and the kitchen. During the first few weeks that she came from the Hospital, I teased her often about being a bush girl because she seemed so intensely interested in things which I had always taken for granted.

I began joining Motunrayo in the kitchen and we were talking freely. I brought the subject of her parents up and we talked at length. She told me the story of her life and everything I needed to know about her.

During those talks, I learned about her childhood and I came to understand the ambition her father had instilled in her when she was a child. I realized that she wasn't really joking when she said she wanted to be a legal practitioner... a Lawyer! She was a very intelligent girl and a good listener too who would think deeply before forming her own opinion on any matter. I gathered that even as a child she was brilliant, quick witted and responsible.

One quiet evening, after we had a sumptuous meal, Motunrayo asked when she would return to her room at the Boys' Quarters (BQ);

"*Oga*... When am I moving back to my room at the Boys' Quarters?" She asked innocently. "I am quite okay now", she said.

The question came to me as a shock. I thought she was enjoying her stay with me. Moreover, I accorded her all the respect a lady deserved not considering the fact that she came to serve as a housekeeper in my house.

"You will move back whenever I say so. Are you tired of being in the main building here?"

"No Sir...! It is just that I want to get back to the routine of work, now that I am well." She smiled bravely.

"Hmmm... It is the Doctor that will declare you fit and sound. Until then, you would be under my nose for surveillance." I laughed.

"Under your nose...?" She squeezed her nose.

"Yes....under my supervision, I mean. Any objection...?" I opened my palms.

We didn't talk about her moving back to the BQ again. I was enjoying her presence and I didn't feel lonely any longer. I now looked forward to coming home to meet someone at home. We started having a family altar and praying together. I liked her very much for who she was and I had started growing fond of her.

One day, I decided to go and meet her parents in their home town. I felt it was not right to keep a young girl in the house without knowing her root. I didn't want a repeat of what happened the other day when she got ill and had to be admitted in the hospital.

I took time off for the journey. We traveled to Saki with gifts, foodstuff and clothes. Her relations were happy to receive us. They greeted her with the admiring respect that came with a car owner. I told her father I came to show up as his daughter's guardian and also to know who the girl's parents were. However, we were well entertained within their limit.

After a long while of chatting, the father called me into a room for a private talk. He was picking his words carefully and he asked about my status and I told him that my wife had left me. He said he would like to give me his daughter Motunrayo to marry. I was shocked!

Such a thought had never crossed my mind. Did I look like a potential husband to the old man? Or did he think his daughter brought me here for introduction formalities? Why wouldn't he think like that, when we had packaged so many foodstuff and gifts for him? By the way, the girl was too young for me to marry. At that time, I was 55years old and the girl was about 22years old. The old man told me to think about it.

As a matter of fact, I had nothing to think about. Linda my ex-wife had spent 28 years of her life with me and we did not have a pleasure of a conjugal enjoyment for a single day; would I now suppress this innocent girl from her prime age to go through unnecessary stress?

No, I still have not forgotten the parting words of Linda, who thought I deliberately put her under bondage of barrenness. Anyway, the divorce proceeding started and we were finally and officially divorced.

It would be safer for me to move on with my life than to tag an innocent girl along. The fact still remains that she came to serve as a house maid, even though I tried to wipe that fact off my mind.

On our way back to Ibadan, we had to stop over at several places. Motunrayo wanted us to greet her relatives and friends in some of the smaller towns along the route from Saki town. We stopped at Ago-Are, her Mother's home town to greet her uncles and aunties. She went happily round some houses to greet them. Other towns we went were Sabe, Agunrege, Okaka and Ipapo.

At each of these smaller towns, Motunrayo took me round and excitedly introduced me as her *Oga* ...her boss. The way she called the boss was quite endearing; her eyes lit up lovingly and there was a kind of sweet looks she gave me. She happily told whoever cared to listen that I was really taking good care of her. She whirled round to display her frame.

She walked with an air of importance; her shoulders were held high. Her friends surrounded her and she was behaving like a

"Birthday girl" who was prepared to share her cake with them. I never knew that side of Motunrayo at all. I didn't know her to be so talkative. She exaggerated on the care I gave her.

I glanced at her audience and I realized that they had another representation of me. To them, they saw a husband that Motunrayo had brought home to show them. I was sure this was not what the girl had in mind because at home I didn't give her the grounds to feel that way.

There must be a reason or reasons for this hyper excited mode she put up. I must remember to ask her later, I said within me but I decided to play along and I was smiling at everyone nicely and giving them money.

Her family and friends came round the car to see us off and to admire the big 4wheeled Infinity jeep that we drove there. Before we left, they all chorused that I should take good care of their friend and sister while some of them winked at me knowingly. I smiled yet again without saying anything.

Motunrayo promised all of them that we would come around again soon to visit them.

As soon as we hit the road, I commended the girl for being a great actress;

"You didn't tell me you are a great actress, Motunrayo. The way you displayed over there, one would think you are a member of a Theatre group." I said.

"Me? Acting as how, Sir?" She feigned innocence.

"Emm....I mean, like the way you were showing me off as your boss." I answered.

"You are my boss, Sir, aren't you?" She spread her hands.

"Did you realize how many towns and villages we had stopped to greet people? Was it actually to greet them or to show off?" I asked sternly.

She was silent, staring at me, with her lips working as if she had something to say. I didn't know whether to laugh or to smile. Then she said abruptly;

"Don't say that, *Oga*!" She turned her head away to suppress a smile.

"Don't say what?"

"Sir, I am sorry I didn't put you in the know, before we got there. I did it on purpose. As a matter of fact, I wanted them to see that the Lord has lifted me up. All of them in each of the places we went were so cruel to me over the years. I was happy they saw that I stepped out of a nice big Jeep vehicle and that I sat in the front seat beside you. The fact that you gave them plenty of money at each of the houses we visited thrilled me to high heavens." She beamed at the remembrance.

"Hmmmm....I see!" was all I could say!

"Sir, I must thank you for playing along", she said softly.

"Did I...? Oh, was I in your script too? What role did you cast me?"

"No role Sir. I am only happy you didn't tell them who I really am. I mean you didn't tell them that I am your house girl." She said.

"What if they get to know someday?" I asked.

"Sir, I left our town about many years ago. None of them saw or heard of me since then. I had nothing when I was leaving home. I was neglected and psychologically abused. So when this opportunity came to visit, I decided to utilize it and show off. I am sorry if I have embarrassed you, Sir." She said pleadingly.

"You have given them something to discuss for the next few days." I couldn't help myself saying it.

"...For few days *keh?* For the next few months I would be the topic of their discussion!" She said excitedly.

We became quiet; each of us in our thoughts. I looked at Motunrayo who had a contented smile on her face and a faraway look. She looked so happy. I suddenly felt an incredible closeness to her. It was a good thing we proposed to visit her family. I would be able to relate with her in a more dignified way, now that I know her family.

Looking at her at times, I was made to remember my horrible past as a glorified houseboy in Big Brother's house. Would I ever forget those awful years? Anyway, God is my vindicator. Time, they say is a great healer of psychological wounds. How true is this, as far as I am concerned?

Chapter 14

The Great Deliverance

Life was back to normal at home. Motunrayo had integrated herself into the system of a housekeeper that lived within the main building. It had been two years and a few months now since Linda left me. I kept putting on a brave face before friends and family who asked of her; I told them she travelled. How much longer would I continue to hide behind one finger?

I had a regimented life of going to work and coming home to surf the internet. One day, I read an article that someone posted online with a hilarious illustration. I laughed out so loudly that Motunrayo ran from the kitchen to the living room where I sat; her hands dripping of water and she was wiping them on the apron she wore.

"*Oga*... I hope all is well." She said.

"Come...come and read this yourself". I beckoned to her and tapped the seat next to me for her to sit.

She did and pierced through the screen. She read what I showed her to read and started laughing too. To stable herself she held one of my knees for support. As she did this, I felt a very painful sharp stab in my groin. Almost immediately, I let out a very loud painful shriek and I held my groins. Motunrayo on her part stood up like a flash and ran towards the kitchen before pausing to look back at me;

"*Oga*, what happened...what is the matter with you?" She raised her eyebrows sympathetically. Her eyes nearly popped out of her socket. She was greatly shaken.

I could not reply her. The excruciating pain made me to be in shock. I just opened my mouth with no words coming out and I didn't remove my eyes from Motunrayo. I was transfixed to the same spot. She kept on asking me if I was alright, but I didn't respond. She rushed to the kitchen and brought back a glass of water from the water dispenser. I was just staring at her.

For what seem like eternity, I just held on to my groin. Suddenly I shouted, "Praise the Lord..."!!! I shouted in a very loud voice that nearly shook the foundation of the house. I stood up as if I wanted to attack an enemy and I rushed to the wall and was banging it. I wasn't banging for the fun of it; I was weeping, praising and thanking God for deliverance!

Poor Motunrayo, she didn't know what got into me, but she went on her knees and joined me in thanking God. I could hear her voice in praises to God. We were there for two hours, just praising the King of kings and the Lord of lords; it was awesome! The heavens really opened!

I was panting from the exercise and kept on shaking my head and the tears would not stop flowing, it was a very emotional scene as I came back to my seat. I called Motunrayo to come nearer and sit beside me. She moved with trepidation and sat far away.

I waved her nearer then I touched her again. The piercing pain was not as pronounced as the first time. I took her hands and hugged her tightly with endearment. It was my innocent way of saying 'Thank you'!

The girl flew away as if an ant had bitten her bum. She rushed to the kitchen shutting the door in what was almost a slam behind her. I was short of words! I went to the door and called her name several times to open the door which she refused.

Back at the living room, I sat down and held my head in my arms. I was choked with tears. Tears of joy were dripping from my eyes. For well over 30years, I didn't have any feelings whatsoever from my groin until this girl innocently placed her hand on my knee. Was I dreaming? What a fundamental miracle!

When she eventually opened the door, her eyes were red from crying. I called her nearer but she sat down far from me. I didn't mind and I told her the story of my life; I was willing to tell it all. I didn't forget to include the reason why Linda left me.

All through the time I was pouring my heart to Motunrayo, she did a remarkable thing; she didn't play a judge over my life. She only listened and didn't say a word; she looked at me for a while as if deciding whether or not to believe me.

After a while, she stood up to set the table for food. I didn't feel like eating though; I was too elated to eat but she insisted in a very stern voice like a mother would do, urging her son to finish his vegetable. She had never used that tone on me before. It was like she was in charge!

We had our dinner in silence. I ate a little and looked across the table at Motunrayo who had concentrated on her food as if she was studying for an exam. She raised her head up suddenly;

"*Oga*, I don't like to speak to you in this tone, but I am bound to tell you that you have to eat to have the strength to hold yourself."

Her voice sounded as though it belonged to someone else or maybe as though she were in an echo chamber. I gave her a sullen glare.

"That's your opinion, isn't it?"

"Yes, it is indeed, *Oga*.

I obeyed and we ate our meal in silence and without tantrums. After dinner we sat together and she poured out her heart about the sibling rivalry in her family too which made her to escape from home with her sanity intact. I could relate with her story because I had been in that voyage once upon a long time.

The following day was a weekend. I took her out for shopping. It was my way of showing appreciation to her. With a child's excitement in her eyes she went about the Shopping Mall pointing at what fascinated her and picking things and asking if she could have them. I paid for anything she had always wanted to have; Android phone, shoes, gowns, tops, jeans, earrings, necklaces and make-up kit.

I obliged her to have an open cheque to buy whatever caught her fancy. Her shopping trolley was full to the brim. I even stayed with her at the hair dresser's salon to relax and fix her hair and nails.

We also went to the cinema and a nice Restaurant for our dinner. From that point, we hit it off. We laughed, we joked and there was some kind of definite chemistry between us. We spent the whole day outdoors and we didn't return until late at night. I was so fagged out that I slept off on the rug after barely watching the news for ten minutes.

Motunrayo had gone to put on one of the dresses I bought for her to show me. She woke me up and I saw a transformation in the girl I once regarded as my housemaid. She was radiantly beautiful. One look at her face threw me off balance!

"Wow... You are gorgeous!" I whispered.

"Thank you Sir." She smiled.

The sweet smile she gave me was doing strange things to my insides. It was as if I had never seen her smile before. There was an awkward pause. Finally, I tried to laugh as if I really had noticed nothing in her dressing but as much as I tried, I couldn't control my feelings any longer.

My body began to vibrate with desire. I wanted her but my other mind was reminding me of the girl's status in my house! However, I tried to keep my mental arrangement intact but other thoughts insisted on breaking it up. I remembered the day I had my groove back. Nothing would ever erase that time from my memories. There was a rush of silence between us and I could not remove my eyes from her.

If it was a dream, I didn't want to wake up. I propped myself up and held her chin in my hand. She wanted to talk but I silenced her by placing a finger across her lips. I studied her face intently.

A surge of passion overwhelmed me; I was breathing laboriously. I moaned loudly and pulled her to me. With the lipstick and all, I gave her a sizzling kiss and I couldn't control myself any longer. She groaned softly, an extra ordinary sound that seemed like an agony of delight. In other words, I deflowered her with a feeble resistance from her. It was a nice experience after over 30years of impotency! I felt the tension easing out of my body.

Motunrayo's status changed from that day; from my house-maid to my bed-mate and she packed into my room where I had an uninterrupted access to enjoy her love and exploration to the fullest.

I had never thought in my wildest dream that I would touch or see the girl's nakedness. Before now, she was simply the house-maid and I saw her that way all the time! However, I fell in love with my Housemaid.

Yes...My house-maid... What about it? What is the big deal...? They do say you find love when you least expect it. Now, I believe in second chance at life. On more than one occasion, I was the recipient of her love and concern. I bless the day she found her way into our house... I bless the day I got my groove back... the day the scales fell from my eyes and I saw she was the woman for me.

Everly Brothers' song- ***I Bless the Day I Found You****;* captured my feelings of all times.

Chapter 15

These Are My Scars!

I had told Gbenga Onilari those same words sometime ago, "Yes...My house-maid... What about it? What is the big deal...?" It was when he came on a visit one day and met Motunrayo and I alone in the house watching TV. This was before I had my groove back. At that time, she was nothing to me but my housemaid.

Gbenga was one of my childhood friends whom we shared secrets and heartfelt things together. Motunrayo served him drinks and excused herself to give us space to talk. When she was away from earshot, Gbenga winked at me and said two and two will always be two. He raised his glass and made a toast.

"To the smartest guy I have ever met; eating his cake and having it", he laughed heartily.

"What do you mean, you this naughty fellow?" I feigned an angry mode.

"I am serious, Abayor, I think you and that girl; your housemaid, I mean... are in love". Gbenga said.

I looked up, surprised. "What's that supposed to mean?"

"Well, I may be wrong, but from the look of things, I can sense an affair a mile away". Gbenga looked so serious.

"So, because she is a young girl, you are having a sense of feeling. What if I had hired an old woman, you wouldn't have said a word, would you?" I smiled faintly and shook my head.

Gbenga looked around and whispered. "I hope you are not sleeping with her, Abayor?"

"What if I am?" I spoke angrily this time.

"...Because it is not good for your status." He replied.

Looking at Gbenga in the eye, I answered. "Okay, she is my housemaid. Yes...My housemaid...and bed-mate! Okay? What about it? What is the big deal...?"

Gbenga thought I had lost my mind to have said that.

"Don't play with fire, Abayor; you may not be able to handle it". Gbenga shrugged his shoulders.

That was the wrong impression that my friend had about Motunrayo and I, some months before then. He would feel vindicated that he told me of his sense of feeling. At that time, I didn't see the girl as anything except as a maid. I often told myself that Mount Everest would shrink to a molehill before I could love my housemaid. Well, Mount Everest had just shrunk!

A month had passed before Motunrayo solemnly told me over breakfast one day that she had something important to tell me. It was an ordinary morning of an ordinary day. She looked up from her plate as if she was caught being naughty, and then her face fractured into a hundred little lines of pain.

She spoke to me with seriousness rare even to her. Adrenaline pounded through my veins. My heart started racing like I had played the championship game. All sorts of bad thoughts crossed my mind; maybe she would tell me she was going back to her parents or what could it be? I felt a sudden sense of awkwardness.

This was a girl I had grown to love over the months, who had shared my bed, just as I have shared hers. I didn't understand the look on her face at that moment.

"Motunrayo, what is it? Tell me." My voice sounded as if I was being strangled. I felt an ache in my stomach. My mind was in turmoil for minutes.

There was a long pause and it was as if Motunrayo was taking a breath, trying to find courage to say what was on her mind. She stared at her food and blew out her cheek.

"It is just that it is complicated.... I mean, I am....emmm..."

There was another long pause, and again I had the feeling that she was weighing up words, testing them for strength. All of a sudden her words came out in a rush and I listened to her;

"I have missed my period"! She blurted out and couldn't meet my eyes.

All my anxieties flew out of the window. "Say it again... Are you sure?"

She nodded but couldn't look at me. There was no time to sit or linger over breakfast after hearing the news. I rose up quickly and hurried her up to get ready to go to the hospital for confirmation. It was confirmed that Motunrayo was six weeks gone.

Let me confess to you, *Yinkus mi...*, I was highly elated. Tears were shed; emotions ran wild and I was just grateful to God. The news had lifted my self esteem. I didn't know what to do again; I was standing and sitting almost at the same time. I could not believe my ears that I, Abayomi Durogbajo would soon be a father for the first time at 57years old when all hopes had been lost of ever tasting the ecstasy of fatherhood. I would have given anything I possessed to have a taste of it. I have been humbled by all the pains I went through.

I pampered Motunrayo to a fault. I didn't allow her to do any household chores. I would rub her back and rub her legs every evening. Oh, the feeling was delightful. I was so joyful that I could not hide it.

I screwed up my courage and asked Motunrayo if she would marry me. She smiled shyly and nodded her head. I was sure she felt as if she was in a dream world.

Motunrayo... A girl, who was once-upon-a-time my house maid, was now acquiring a new status. Before Motunrayo's child delivery I had sent words to her father, confirming his desire to give me his daughter as a wife.

"She is all yours for keeps. Just take good care of her." The elderly man told me over the phone. I planned to do a very private traditional marriage and I put preparation into gear. I also decided to change Motunrayo's name. That name to me, was synonymous to her being my house-maid. I wanted a clean fresh start with a woman that I loved, a woman that I deflowered.

She metamorphosed into my wife. I gave her a new name as Tunmise. It means "I am renewed". Indeed I am renewed and reborn. To us, Motunrayo is dead. Tunmise has come to stay. I have not regretted my actions since then.

Her picture takes a pride of place in the display of pictures in the living-room as you can see. I wanted to be with her all the time. You might want to say that I am a man blinded with love goggles; yes, I am.

We spent the next several weeks together, just hanging around; talking about everything under the sun. We had the whole world to ourselves. It was wonderful...! Some evenings we went to dinner at different five star Hotels and Restaurants.

Tunmise loved the glitter and the ways the waiters were hovering nearby. She once asked me to explain to her which cutlery goes with what food. I didn't know whether to laugh or be properly penitent when she told me seriously:

"I must know all about these things if I am to be your wife, *Oga*. So please don't tease me when I ask what may seem to be silly questions."

I simply smiled. Her face would glow with happiness and she would lean across to me and whisper:

"I love you, *Oga*!"

Anyone who had been in love would understand how we felt for each other. We lived in our own world where we saw the universe in each other's eyes. We had our intimate times, exclusive, isolated from everyday events around us.

Weeks went by, and months climbed over months. We had a small wedding at a Marriage Registry and Tunmise became my legal wife and we were living in bliss in our own small world. I must mention that she still calls me *Oga* till today. I have tried to wean her off it but she would not stop. So, I let her be.

I didn't know I could still smile. Ever since Linda left me, my self confidence took a major nose-dive. However, marrying this girl had given me back my confidence. Sometimes, it is better to move on in life than to sulk. For years, I suffered from a long battle with panic attacks but now I have weaned myself from it with the help of constant counseling and my determination to move on.

You see, anyone hearing my story would be quick to judge that I took advantage of the poor girl. I like to always say that some things cannot be explained, except you go through them.

To confess to you, I grew fond of her since she came back from the hospital, the time she was ill. I liked her; the more we talked, the more I liked her but I never thought she would one day be my wife. The thoughts never crossed my mind.

*Yinkus mi....*The lady that you met earlier in this house was that housemaid. Her mind is as sharp as a knife. She may seem to you as a gentle, vulnerable girl but underneath the gentle mien is a smart, tough, resilient, responsible and passionate lovely woman.

She makes me happy daily and I have no regret in my decision to make her my wife. I have been married to her for about five years now. I love my wife and she loves me too. I enjoy being with her. To have a spouse that loves you is a remarkable gift.

To crown my joy, God gave us twins; both are boys! I was obsessed by the arrival of the twins when they were born. I was always checking on them constantly. I was enthralled and I spent most of my spare time watching them. This explains the gap in our age group. I have my wife and I have my children!

Yinkus mi.... The snare is broken and I have escaped. I am a bundle of miracle going somewhere to happen. I strongly believe that we are not defined by our past but by God's purpose. I am standing in grace. The troubles I have gone through, my children will not repeat it in Jesus name.

The badly written scripts of my life will never play out on my children again. All along, I knew God had a bigger plan for me and what I was going through at that time was a phase but I couldn't figure how God would do it or how He would bring it into fruition. This song captures how I felt;

Thank you, Lord, for Your Blessings ... by Jeff & Sheri Easter.

"...You gave me your love Lord

And a fine family; thank you Lord

For your blessings on me"!

Chapter 16

Where There Is A Will...

Yinkus mi.... You might want to ask what Big Brother had said when I was going through my travails. To my mind, I felt like he was happy to see me in pains. The fact that I am now successful in life gives him heart burn. And the fact that I left his house many years ago and I am well established on my own did not remove anything from him. He simply could not handle it.

He wanted to copy everything I did and wanted to buy everything I bought. And if he was unable to replicate anything from me, he was sure to bad-mouth me in the presence of a crowd. He was always talking about me, trying to make me look bad.

He still sees me as his "that stupid little brother" and I in return see him as "the ruthless and domineering Big Brother with wicked monitoring eyes". We still meet at family functions from time to time but on a good number of the times, I run away from such parties to avoid coming in contact with him because he would want to disgrace me in public.

What is worrisome about Big Brother is that he is a man so unpredictable, so reckless to do evil to me and so full of blind self-regard. His obsession to pull me down; his determination to see my end; his craving for revenge on me is well known to our extended family till date. He wields unimaginable power and he is using it to its maximum capacity.

I can liken him to a pig that is sunk in the mud and squealing with shameless pleasure. He has demeaned me a number of times at family gatherings and has lashed out on me, declaring me his number one arch-enemy. Big Brother's deep hatred and contempt for seeing me excel is palpable. His utter lack of regard for elders in the family who try wading in-between us is shameful.

The most painful thing to me is his two children who had hitherto been my high flying supporters when they were younger have now sworn to keep sides with their father. He is encouraging his children to disrespect me and join forces with him to fight on. This was a conflict that started before those children were born.

It is not clear whether I actually offended him or not because for over forty five years down the line, he is still hammering to whoever cared to listen that I had offended him greatly.

Do you know that the worst psychological disease anyone can breed is the one that has twisted a man's mind into imagining everyone is an enemy? I don't think Big Brother can get over it. It is embedded in him. He is wicked, arrogant and deadly in equal measure.

Many times I have asked myself "when will all this internal strife come to an end"? The simple answer I have for it at the moment is, "only God knows", now that his children are supporting him. I brazed up one day to say that I will survive these hostilities with or without anybody's input.

Let me tell you this, *Yinkus mi*...when something itches, you will either keep scratching it or you find the cause of the itch. It took me years to discover that Big Brother was actually a coward, so I decided to tackle him at his weak point of the game.

What happened was that I took a positive step to free myself. I had planned to have Big Brother ridiculed any time we met again at the family's get-together. I wanted him to have a taste of his own medicine and to hurt him the way I'd been hurt while I was living with him. I wanted to give him his own pound of flesh. I rehearsed in my mind the words which I would splash on his face which would hurt him to his bone marrow if he dared to make a mockery of me again in public.

I actually told him off that day. We met at a family gathering and as he was about to repeat his act of antagonism, I rose up to confront him. I gave him the full dose of animosity. He was shocked and I warned him to steer clear of me in the future. No one at that party could intervene because they had been hinting that I was the only one who could help myself and deal with the old bully of a brother whose second nature was anger! I think insecurity is his number two vice.

It is important to note that if you have people around you who are constantly pulling you down, bad-mouthing you, telling you what you can't do and saying you will never accomplish your dreams in life, it is better to show them the way out; separate yourself from them. You don't need that poison in your life. If you continue to hang out with them, you will be defeated.

I structured my pattern of thinking not to tolerate Big Brother's manipulation and intimidation any longer. I made up my mind to move on with my life and I have worked on my self esteem and positive affirmations. I resolved to stay positive and stay productive. I had to start writing my thoughts and feelings down as poems. That has helped me in developing my inner strength.

Let me say here that quarrels or disagreements are normal in sibling relationships but when it is evident that such conflicts could be life threatening, it is better to sever such relationships once and for all.

That was exactly what I did. When I was at the brink of losing my sanity I reached out to the elderly man that pulled me out of the Dam the time I was about to commit suicide. I was always going to him for counseling.

With the touch of God in my hand, I was able to navigate the dark tunnel. As the saying goes, there is light at the end of the tunnel. When I think back to those vulnerable days when Big Brother pushed me back and forth, I hardly believed I went through all that I did.

The good news and the consoling part is that I survived because God has the final say over my life. I have experienced the repercussion of running with the wrong crowd when I was at the University and now I am healed.

As I moved on with my life, I had to contend with the snide remarks of those individuals who were too quick to rub insults to my injury. They heard that Linda had left me, yet they would come round to pretend that they were concerned about my affair. I never let them get past the first question when they asked me where my wife was. I looked at them in the face and just say an incoherent babbling, "Yum... yum... yum... yum...!" That usually shuts them up because I had not said anything!

Yinkus mi... I must really appreciate you for being a very good listener. My lines of thought would have been disrupted if you had voiced out something or derailed my concentration by interrupting me. Wow...! Each time I expressed my painful experiences as I just did, I feel light but it is not everyone you can call to listen to your story.

We all have emotional scars that we keep from the public. You have yours and I have mine. So, these are my scars; my healed wounds, my scratch marks all splashed on me in different colors. I thank God I am a survivor today. It could only have been God. Talking about it now is such a relief. Those were the years I journeyed through the dark and dreary tunnel. *Yinkus mi...* Thank you for hearing me out. You can take the floor now. Over to you...!

****

Abayomi Durogbajo took a long swig at his wine and stretched his legs to the full length of his frame. It was a way to signify the end of his story. He wiped his mouth with a napkin and stared into the air.

I detected certain inflexibility in his voice and he lost his looks as he was rounding up his story. It was a tear jerk and a heart breaking look on the tortured side of a man who rose from nothing to a genius.

****

Abayor and I were both quiet for what seemed like hours; each of us in our own thoughts. It was so pleasant just to sit there and look into space! Abayor's story feels a bit like a documentary of my own family history. It was so apt and concise! Just like him, I was orphaned early in life by fate and I am determined to survive and achieve great endeavours in life.

"Abayor...," I started. "Congratulations! You are a go-getter and I dare say you've missed your calling. You should have turned to acting or story-telling as a career. Do you know that your story has really inspired me? It has given me a new lease of life that, where there is a will, there is a way.

Someone out there waits to be inspired by your story. I'm so happy for you, Abayor! You deserve the happiness after all you've been through. I must say you narrated it so well that one would think you read Arts at School!"

"Hmmm...." This was all Abayor could say. His voice was barely audible as he answered. I knew what he meant.

He kept on staring into space. Probably he was trying to relive the activities all over again in his head. He held up his glass cup. His fingers were playing with the rim of the cup, back and forth. My glance went from Abayor to the wall clock and back to Abayor again. He must have read my thoughts. He hurriedly gulped all his drink. I stood up immediately and stretched my back.

"It's been nice being in your company, Abayor. Talking with you is an education in itself." I said as I moved to the window to view the serene atmosphere of his garden.

I realized that the day was far spent and I needed to be home before my husband, FM returns from his Old Boys Association meeting.

Abayor stood up and impulsively hugged me from behind, around the waist and buried his head in my back for a few moments. He then moved to stand beside me at the window sill. I suppressed a desire to put my arms around him and give him a brotherly bear hug. Instead, I put out my hand with a grin and I gave him a gentle hand squeeze.

"Thank you, *Yinkus mi.* I have enjoyed your company enormously even though I was the one that did all the talking." Abayor cooed into my ears softly with a smile.

I was silent, my mind in turmoil. Mostly I was feeling a kind of embarrassment with myself for acting like a love-sick teenager. I shouldn't have allowed him to hug me from the back.

"We are both married now, you know." I pointed to my ring and he gave me a watery smile. We were then quiet for a few minutes.

"I could do something about your story, you know? I mean I could publish it in a book. I would want the public to learn from it. Do you still write, Abayor?" I asked, trying to feel normal.

"Yes I still do. I enjoy writing. I write under a pseudonym."

"I see..." I said. "You were a prolific writer when we were on Campus. Were you not on the Editorial Board of the hottest magazine on Campus...? What's the name again?" I asked. Abayor smiled widely and exclaimed, "Yinkaaaa...! You don't tell me you have forgotten its name upon all the fights some of us put up for you when one of the reporters of the magazine wanted to victimize you, just because you turned down his advances."

I tried to remember the incident he was referring to, but I couldn't. It must have been in the trash bin of my memory computer. I usually delete unpleasant memories from my internal brain storage. I wonder why Abayor was able to still remember every detailed occurrence of his life.

It seemed like there was a computer database in his head. It was so fresh that as I listened to him, I could vividly capture the events unfolding before my eyes. He depicted it so well that I felt I was present through all the plots of the story of his life.

"By the way, Abayor, we do not become weak by forgiving people. Have you forgiven him?"

"Who...?"

"Your Big Brother of course...! Who else...?"

"Years ago...!" Abayor snapped his finger backward to show it happened a long time ago. "I have forgiven him quite alright in my heart, but he hasn't forgiven me, though. He is a man with the pride of a Lucifer. I still visit him once in a long while if there was a need for it, most especially if there was a family meeting but I don't make a pilgrimage out of it. His resentment for me is legendary"

"So, what are you planning to do about it?" I asked.

"Nothing...! Absolutely nothing! He has a case to answer with his Maker when he eventually dies. I can stand for a lot of things but I can't stand for those who treat me unkindly. I am home and dry!"

He raised his two hands up as a supplication to God. There was a significant pause.

****

Abayor and his wife saw me off to my car. I hugged them both and I slipped in behind the wheels. By this time, the twilight was set and shone at the windscreen of my car. We said our goodbyes and I waved to them.

Wow! What an evening to remember in a long time! What Abayor failed to realize is that, sibling rivalry is as old as it can be.

Stories abound in the Bible of siblings who were jealous of each other or one another. There were those who died in the process-Cain and Abel Story. There were those who survived--Moses and his siblings; Esau and Jacob; Joseph and his Brothers, just to mention a few.

In all homes, we have sibling rivalry. Many did not survive to tell their stories as Abayomi Durogbajo had done; many went with the tide. Those of us who survived it should really thank God for going into the lion's den and coming out unscathed. We need to appreciate and celebrate each other's strength, even as we understand and tolerate each other's weaknesses. Let us be bold to conquer our fears and face our lions!

Do I really wish to tell my own story as Abayor had done and make it public? Hmmm...Time will tell. I have a story to tell too. But who would be keen to listen to me? Foolish angry tears were stinging my eyes as I remember all I have been through too, in the hands of an elder Sister...those years that I lived in fear of her!

Chapter 17

You Can Count On Me

I switched on the car stereo and it was the music of King Sunny Ade, the juju beat maestro that was blaring in the cool evening. I sang along with him as I sped home.

Darkness was falling now. I only wish FM would not get home before me! Let hell not loose! I got to our gate and I realized his car was already packed at its place. His silhouette moved animatedly in the half-light. He had been waiting for me under the canopy at a corner on the lawn!

It is his favorite place for fresh air if he doesn't want to sit indoors. For instance, after his early morning walk within our estate, FM would sit outside as if he is communing with the sky and the clouds and think his own thoughts...those are his private moments!

Talk about feeling jittery to my roots. I felt "guilt" must be written all over my face. Come to think of it, why should I feel guilty at visiting an old friend? But I was silent. Mostly I was feeling a kind of embarrassment with myself for acting like a love-sick teenager.

I got down from the car and stood by it, not moving an inch. FM turned and was coming towards me without talking. I was unprepared for his reactions. He came to me and took my hands in his, scrutinizing my face as if he could not believe it was me and then hugged me tightly. His voice was choked and he looked tired and worried. His voice came in mild rebuke as he lamented and wanted to know where I went.

"Where have you been all day, my darling? I was a bit worried when I came home some hours ago and I didn't meet you. Where were you for hours?"

I gave a watery smile and could not meet his eyes. I later glanced at him before replying. He was gazing steadily at me, his eyes narrowed and speculative. He seemed to be waiting for more than an answer to his questions.

I tried to ask him about the Old Boys Association he went to attend but he put a finger on my lips and told me how he changed his mind to visit an old friend he met during the week. It was his third time of visiting his house. He said after staying with him for about 30minutes today, he got tired of his presence and wanted to come home to me.

"I just wanted to come back to you but you were not indoors either. I couldn't contact you on phone! Where were you, *Sisi mi?*" FM's question was whispered, scarcely audible.

FM wanted to know with a dissembling smile. I liked the way his mouth remained mobile after he had spoken the first few words, as if there were more to come. Perhaps he sensed my thoughts, because he stared at me for a moment and then looked away. We were silent for a few minutes. To answer his question, I bloated out;

"I am home now. Let's just forget about everything that happened today, okay? We have each other now and that's the ultimate!"

I laughed uncomfortably and it was accompanied by a gentle nod of agreement from my husband. I knew my answer lacked conviction and I hurriedly gave him a quick hug. Perhaps FM sensed my thoughts, because he stared at me for a moment and then turned again towards the gate. I really wish I knew how to put my feelings about the whole scenario into words.

I remembered how Abayor had been fiddling with the rim of his wine glass cup and staring into space. You see, meeting my old friend, Abayor made me to relive my younger days when I was blossoming and carefree. As far as I could tell, I thought I had lost my bloom, but now I think my bloom is back in place!

Inside me right now, I feel like a young girl again but I am not young. I am a fully fledged grandmother, complete with rescinding hairline and wrinkles; not forgetting that I have thirty-three years down the line of marital journey. Where has the time gone? How time flies? Sometimes in life, we get thoroughly tangled with what we did not bargain for and all we need to do is to patiently look inwards and make amends before it is too late to make a detour.

By now, my husband was looking a bit shell-shocked. He looked at me suddenly as if he had just found the words. And I thought I knew what was going on in his mind. He wanted to tell me how sorry he was about something.

Whatever FM met where he went had engulfed him. I held his hands and kissed them. His hand reached over to cover mine. He understood and for a second or two, I actually felt the earth moved. Impulsively, I placed my head on his chest. I synchronized with the rhythm beating of his heart. This is my place! This is where I belong to. What more could I ask for?

For a long quiet moment I looked up at my husband and I thought; "this man has integrity, honesty and guts. He is very sensitive too. Oh, how I loved him". I said within me. He is my Knight in shining armor. His troubled, questioning expression changed suddenly into a broad smile. Obviously he was satisfied at what he saw on my face. No more stories!

I was glad I never had the chance to tell FM about Abayor. He might not understand the chemistry between two old friends! I smiled at my husband; there was a lump in my throat. I felt like crying. There are some things that are best kept covered up for the sake of peace! Do you agree with me? I can count on my husband's love for me any day! From the rising of the sun till it's going down, I would always be devoted to him.

DEVOTED TO YOU ... By the Everly Brothers

"Darlin' you can count on me

Till the sun dries up the sea

Until then I'll always be devoted to you...."

Author's Profile

Oluyinka Adetola Adeboye (Nee Adeyefa) is a graduate of the University of Ife now Obafemi Awolowo University Ile-Ife Nigeria.

She obtains a Bachelor of Arts Degree, B.A (Hons) in Yoruba Literature in the Department of African Languages and Literatures.

She also holds a Master's Degree in Communication and Language Arts (MCA) from the University of Ibadan Nigeria.

Yinka Adeboye had worked with the Federal Radio Corporation of Nigeria (FRCN) Ikoyi Lagos Nigeria as an Artiste Producer.

Yinka is an alumnus of the famous "Haggai Nigeria", an affiliation of Haggai Institute for Advanced Leadership Training in Singapore.

She is also an alumnus of several Christian Institutions, including;

*School of Deliverance and Healing, under the auspices of God-will-do it Ministry Ibadan Nigeria;

*The Redeemed Christian Bible College;

*Mount Zion Faith Ministry School of Drama: to mention a few, all in Nigeria.

Yinka Adeboye is the Author of a Yoruba Novel, titled; O SOJU MI. This is a fiction novel on the biography of an account of the grace of God in one of the struggling moments a woman could go through.

She is also the Author of many English titled books. Amongst them are;

*RUMBLINGS OF MY INNER THOUGHTS (Poetry)

*GOD: A CONSUMING FIRE

*IT IS SO LONG

*LEMON WITH PRIDE

*ENTANGLED WEB (A Play)

*SELECTED AFRICAN STORIES MY GRANDMOTHER TOLD ME

Yinka is a member of so many associations, they include:

*Association of Nigerian Authors (ANA) Oyo State Branch

*A Fellow of the Famous Ebedi International Writers' Residency in Iseyin, Nigeria.

*Ibadan Poetry Enclave;

*National Association of Yoruba Creative Writers (Egbe Onkowe Yoruba);

*Association of Teachers of the Yoruba Language and Culture of Nigeria (Egbe Akomolede Ati Asa Naijiria)

Yinka is currently the Vice-Chairperson of the Association of Nigerian Authors Oyo State Chapter...2018--

She is also the current Secretary-general of the National Association of Yoruba Creative Writers in Nigeria...2017--

She is a Poet, a Playwright, a freelance Script Writer, an Event Planner and a Master of Ceremony of repute. She is as well a Counselor and also an Author of both English and Yoruba books.

BACK PAGE

In all homes, we have sibling rivalry. Many did not survive to tell their stories as Abayomi Durogbajo had done in this narrative account; many went with the tide. Those of us who survived it should really thank God for going into the lion's den and coming out unscathed.

Many people are of the opinion that same-mother siblings could never be enemies. In fact, they believe that the rope of unity that binds children of the same mother together can never break. From my personal experiences, it has been proven that same-mother sibling relationship could be complex and even become death threatening.

The reader of this story should be able to identify with the intricacies and plots in this fiction. Each page of this book is a journey into the world of adventures and events. It is excellently written and has a fascinating pull that cannot be ignored once the pages are opened.

"**Splashes of Many Colors**" is a book you will enjoy and that would resonate long after completion ...

Printed in Great Britain
by Amazon

49917170R00139